HBJ

Georges Simenon

Translated from the French
by Alastair Hamilton

THE W

A HELEN AND KURT WOLFF BOO

ENICE TRAIN

IARCOURT BRACE JOVANOVICH : New York and London

Library of Congress Cataloging in Publication Data
Simenon, Georges, 1903–
    The Venice train.
    "A Helen and Kurt Wolff book."
    Translation of Le Train de Venise.
    I. Title.
PZ3.S5892Vc   [PQ2637.I53]   843'.9'12   74-5759
ISBN 0-15-193506-8

First American edition

B C D E

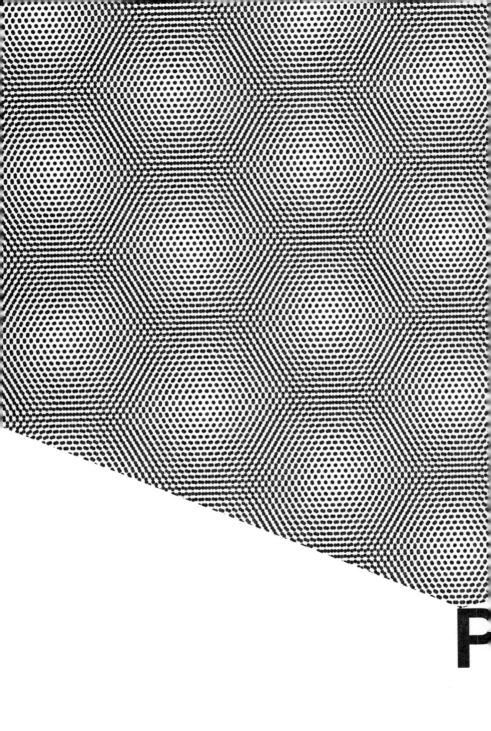

P

ART ONE

Why was the entire image focused on his daughter? This bothered him slightly, though he only really thought about it later, once the train had left, and even then it was no more than a fleeting impression, born to the rhythm of the wheels and promptly absorbed by the landscape.

Why Josée rather than his wife or his son, as they all stood in the damp heat?

Maybe because the figure of his daughter in a railway station, waiting for a train to leave, was more incongruous? She was twelve years old, tall and thin. Her legs and arms were still skinny and the salt water and the sun on the beach had streaked her fair hair with silver.

Just as she was leaving the boardinghouse Dominique had said to her, "You're not going to accompany your father to the station in your bathing suit, are you?"

"Why not? Lots of people take the motorboat in their bathing suits, and the motorboat stops in front of the station. We *are* going swimming immediately afterward, aren't we?"

Dominique was wearing shorts, and one could see the outline of her brassière under the striped blouse she had bought in a crowded little street near a canal whose name he couldn't remember.

Was it the fact that his daughter's breasts were beginning to develop that bothered him?

Everything was hazy, like the morning light, like that sparkling, hot, almost tangible mist.between the water and the sky.

In his limbs and in his head he could still feel the throb of the boat they had caught at the Lido, its regular motion on the long flat waves, its jolts every time it passed another boat.

The view of Venice, all of a sudden, in the early morning heat—the towers, the domes, the palaces, Saint Mark's and the Grand Canal, the gondolas, and, because it was Sunday, the bells ringing from every church, from every campanile.

"May I have an ice cream, Daddy?"

"At eight in the morning?"

"Me too?" asked the little boy, who was only six.

His name was Louis, but ever since his earliest childhood, because of the way he drank his bottle, his parents called him Bib.

Bib was also in his bathing suit, with a checked shirt covering it. The two children were wearing gondoliers' hats, straw hats with flat crowns and brims, a red ribbon for Josée's and a blue one for her brother's.

Basically, perhaps, Calmar did not like being out of his element, and he had been feeling out of his element, without any roots or anything solid to lean on, for fifteen years. It was not he but his wife who had wanted to spend their vacation in Venice, and, of course, the children had agreed enthusiastically.

He hated departures, too, and farewells. He stood at the window of the incongruous compartment, in the only car that had come from beyond Venice, from beyond Trieste. It was a different color than the others; it also looked different and smelled different.

A man already seated in the compartment looked him up and down. He must have been there when it was hitched onto the Venice train.

Calmar did not actually ask himself any precise questions. Unconsciously, rather impatiently, he took in the platform in the yellow light, the newspaper booth in the left-hand corner, other people, to the left and to the right, who were waiting, like his wife and children, their eyes focused on a relative or a friend.

Everything happened as usual. The train was due to leave at 7:54. At 7:52 a man in uniform walked down the platform closing the doors, while a mechanic went from car to car knocking with a hammer. Every time he had ever taken a train Calmar had seen this same performance, and each time he wondered what the man was knocking at with the hammer, but he had always forgotten to inquire.

The stationmaster came out of his office, a whistle between his lips and a red flag rolled like an umbrella in his hand. Steam was spurting out from somewhere or other. It can't have been steam, because the train was electric; yet the breaks were being drained with the same puffs and jolts as in all other trains.

Then, at last, the whistle blew. Josée, who was licking her ice cream—her *gelato,* as she called it now—raised one hand to wave good-by.

"Take care of yourself," said Dominique, "and have all your meals at Étienne's."

Étienne's was a restaurant they knew on Boulevard des Batignolles, a stone's throw from their apartment, where, according to Dominique, the kitchen was clean and the food healthy.

The red flag was unfurled. The stationmaster raised his arm just like Josée and Bib, who was copying her.

The train should have left. The clock stood at 7:55.

But, instead of giving the signal, the stationmaster, who could see the entire train, lowered his arm and gave a series of short and imperious whistles.

The train did not move. The people standing on the platform looked toward the engine. Calmar craned out the window, but all he could see were other heads leaning out, just like his.

"What's happened?"

"I don't know," said Dominique. "I can't see anything out of the ordinary."

She was slim—not as slim as her daughter, of course

—and even in shorts she had a certain elegance. Because she couldn't tan like her children, her skin was simply reddened by the sun, and her blue eyes were hidden behind dark glasses.

The stationmaster, who was now the center of everyone's attention, seemed to be taking his time. His flag under his arm, he was still watching the engine patiently, waiting for God knows what, and the whole station looked like a film that had suddenly been stopped at one frame, a color photograph.

Hands that no longer knew what to do with their handkerchiefs, smiles of farewell that had frozen into grimaces.

"A latecomer?" asked a voice next to Calmar.

"I don't know. I can't see anyone running."

The man, short and thickset, stood up, leaving his newspaper on the seat.

"Do you mind?"

For a second his head and shoulders replaced those of Justin at the window.

"One never knows with the Italians. . . ."

He had had time to see Dominique and the two children. Calmar returned to the window, a forced smile on his lips. He could feel that Josée and Bib were in a hurry to be off, to rush out of this overheated station and jump onto the *vaporetto* that would take them to the beach. Dominique looked anxious and depressed.

"Take care of yourself, Justin."

"I promise."

"I think the train really is leaving now."

It took two more interminable minutes, during which everyone kept his eyes fixed on the indifferent stationmaster.

Finally a deputy stationmaster came out of an office with a glass door and gave a signal. The stationmaster blew his whistle, waited a couple of seconds, and waved his flag. The train moved off. The platform slid back with its rows of figures. Justin leaned farther forward as the figure of his daughter grew smaller and smaller and the red of her bathing suit merged with all the other colors in the station.

The sun grabbed at them, bursting into the compartment along with a gust of burning air; with a sigh, Calmar lowered the blue canvas curtain, which swelled like a sail and flapped up two or three times before settling into place.

They were off.

Settled in his seat, he now had time, even though no particular inclination, to observe his traveling companion, who had crumpled up his newspaper and pushed it under the seat.

For a while the two men pretended not to notice each other. But the stranger seemed in somewhat less of a hurry to turn his eyes away.

He was in late middle age, perhaps fifty-five or sixty. His shoulders were broad, his body powerful, his features firmly chisled.

Calmar had observed that his newspaper was printed in Cyrillic lettering. Russian? Slovenian?

The blue curtain was flapping again, letting the sun in, and this time the other man got up and fixed it, as though he were an expert at it.

"French?" he asked as he sat down again.

"Yes."

"From Paris?"

"Yes."

"I noticed that your wife had a Parisian accent."

Calmar had nothing against starting a conversation, but the opening was always awkward. The train stopped at Venezia Mestre, Venice's other station, and some of the local people passed along the corridors looking for second-class compartments.

"Are you returning ahead of your family for business reasons?"

"We were all supposed to leave today. Unfortunately, there was only one seat available on the 10:32 express. Rather than make my family change at Lausanne and spend the night on the train, I left on my own and let them stay a few days longer, as the children wanted."

He felt that his companion was looking insistently at his lightweight suit, a silk blend with a peppery texture. It was the first time in his life that he had worn such a light-colored suit, a yellowish white, but his wife had insisted he buy it in the same street where she had bought her dresses.

"You're about the only man who's wearing a dark suit, Justin."

He would have preferred to travel in another suit. In Venice or in the boardinghouse it was all right, but here he felt as if he were in disguise. It didn't go with his figure, which was paunchy.

"Enjoy your vacation? Was the weather good?"

"Except for a couple of storms."

"Do you like Italian food?"

"The children love it, except for the shellfish, which my son won't touch. . . ."

"But if you were staying in a boardinghouse you must have had shellfish every day."

He winced. How could this stranger, who had only seen him for a few minutes, guess that they had been staying at a boardinghouse and not at one of the big hotels on the Lido?

He felt slightly humiliated and once more regretted being on the train in his silk and linen suit with its unbecoming Italian cut.

The placid man in the seat facing him began both to irritate and to intrigue him. Surreptitiously, he must have assessed the two suitcases. They had been purchased for the occasion and were not of the best quality. Calmar had once been told that hotel porters judged their clients by their suitcases, just as certain men judge women not by their dress or fur coat, but by their shoes.

"Are you in business?"

"Manufacturing, really, a local industry. But I don't have a firm of my own."

He couldn't help it. In spite of the fact that the other man had no right to interrogate him, he answered with almost scrupulous sincerity.

"Do you mind?" he asked.

He took his jacket off because he was sweating from every pore, despite the wind that blew into the curtain and threatened to unhook it once again. He had large damp patches under his arms and he was ashamed of them, as of a disease. They embarrassed him at the office, too, especially in front of the typists.

"Your daughter will be a beautiful woman."

The man had barely set eyes on her!

"She's very like her mother, but livelier."

It was quite true. What Dominique lacked was spontaneity, what one calls dash. At thirty-two, she was slim, with pleasant features, eyes of a very soft blue, an elegant bearing, but there was always something unobtrusive about her, as though she were afraid of attracting attention, of occupying a more important place than was due her.

"Your wife has a lovely contralto voice."

Justin smiled nervously. How had he noticed all that? It was true that Dominique's voice, solemn and muted, was in contrast with her apparent fragility and consequently sounded especially moving.

Another station already, Padua, the platforms teeming with people, hundreds of people who seemed to be storming the train, a great many children, babies in their mothers' arms, and even a fat peasant woman carrying live chickens in a crate.

People pressed in through every door and pushed through the corridor, knocking into each other in their efforts to find empty seats in the forward carriages.

"You'll see. Soon we won't even be able to get through the corridor."

"Have you taken this train before?"

"Not this one, but others like it. I sometimes wonder where the Italians are shuttling back and forth to with such energy. On some days the entire country seems to be on the move, looking for a place to settle in."

He had an accent that Calmar couldn't place.

"Are you an engineer?"

Once again his question made Calmar start. At least this time he had the satisfaction of knowing his companion to be wrong.

"No. I'm not a technician. I work in the trade division and my particular title—everyone has a title in our firm—is manager of the foreign trade department."

Suddenly the stranger asked in English: "You speak English?" He replied equally in English: "I taught English at the Lycée Carnot."

"You speak German, too?"

"I do."

"Italian?"

"No. Just enough to read the menu in a restaurant."

As the train swayed in a curve in the track, the blue curtain flapped harder than ever and came unfastened again. The ticket collector, who had just come into the compartment, took several minutes to fix it, after which he asked for their tickets.

Calmar's was a plain cardboard rectangle, while the stranger's was a wad of yellow leaves clipped together. The ticket collector detached one leaf and put it into his bag.

Had he been asked, on the train, to assess his impressions, he would have been incapable of analyzing them and no doubt would have answered simply and somewhat grouchily that he was in a hurry to get home.

His reaction would have been the same had he been asked about his vacation. He was fed up with the sun, with the crowds of bathers on the beach, with the racket of the *vaporetti* and *motoscafi*, with Piazza San Marco and its pigeons, with shops where everything seemed so cheap and where one bought useless objects simply because one was away from home. He was fed up, exhausted by all the day and night noises—the songs and the orchestras, the shouts of children, footsteps on the stairs.

Translating the menu at each meal for Josée and her brother and discussing which dishes they were allowed to choose had quickly become an obsession.

And, underlying it all, there was the humiliation of having chosen a boardinghouse without a view of the sea.

And yet he knew that in a few weeks, a few months, a year, the days at the Lido would seem to be among the most luminous and pleasant of his life, and that he would despair of ever reliving something similar again.

This happened every year. It was always the previous year that was marvelous, even the autumn and winter with their flus and children's diseases that worried him so much at the time.

Was this incapacity to be happy other than in retrospect particular to him or was it true of most men? He didn't know and didn't dare ask anybody, least of all his colleagues at the office, who would make fun of him.

At the moment, for instance, he felt ill at ease and counted the hours to Lausanne and then to Paris. To start with, there was the heat, which became increasingly oppressive as the morning drew on. At one point he had opened the door onto the corridor, but since all the windows were open the draft was unbearable.

The curtain had shifted again, but now the rod was so bent that the curtain remained at an angle, leaving a broad ray of sunlight to roast his face.

He could have changed his place. There were four empty seats in the compartment despite the reservation slips above them. The passengers would probably be getting on at one of the next stations.

There was a stop every twenty minutes: Lonigo, San Bonifazio, Verona . . .

The same crowd at each one, the same rush onto the train and the same panic-stricken stampede in the corridors. Soon, however, the stampede stopped because the second-class passengers were hermetically blocking the space outside the compartments. An unusual assortment of baggage took up as much room as the human beings—suitcases fastened by a rope or pieces of string, baskets, cardboard boxes, odd-shaped bundles.

They were all piled higher than the windows, and there were children sitting on the floor. One had to step over them and squeeze past their parents to reach the toilet. After a few more stations, it was impossible even to get there.

And yet nobody tried to occupy those four empty seats, upholstered, comfortable, inviting. Women remained standing, giving a bottle or a breast to a baby, while being shaken about by the train, without even thinking that they could sit down. There was no envy in their eyes, no bitterness or sadness.

"Do you spend your weekends in the country?"

"Near Poissy, yes. Do you know it?"

"It's between Paris and Mantes-la-Jolie, isn't it?"

Actually, the man was not interrogating as much as he was affirming. He gave the impression of knowing the answers in advance, of only asking the questions in order to get a confirmation.

"You have a car?"

"Yes. A *quatre chevaux*. I need it in Paris, especially to go from the office to the factory."

"And you preferred to go by train rather than drive

on those crowded roads. I quite understand, particularly with the children."

And yet they very nearly had gone to Venice by car. It was Josée, of course, who had wanted them to drive, although after fewer than twenty miles she started calculating how long it would take them to arrive.

He had been tempted to go by car himself.

"In that case we'll hardly be able to take any baggage. Less than half of what we each want to take,"— this in Dominique's sensible voice.

"You have a house in the country?"

The other man had no need to mop his brow; there was no sign of sweat on his forehead. From time to time, when the carriage stopped fairly close to the cart selling drinks and snacks—it was usually at the other end of the train—he ordered a small bottle of Campari soda and Calmar ended up by doing the same.

"There's a cart on the train, too, but it won't reach us before Milan."

Deep down, Calmar was becoming irritated by his own docility. He answered all the questions without hedging while, for his part, he didn't dare ask a single one of those that crossed his mind.

For instance, he had observed that his fellow passenger had no baggage in the rack. Were his cases in the baggage van, or did he travel empty-handed?

The carriage came from Belgrade, via Trieste. Under the seat there was a Slavic newspaper. Couldn't he have asked:

"Are you coming from Belgrade?"

Or even:

"Are you a Yugoslav?"

It was unlikely. The stranger didn't look Slavic. His French was as fluent as his English and German, and he spoke to the railroad employees in idiomatic Italian.

He was wearing a nondescript suit of dark, almost

black wool, not particularly well cut. His tie, which he felt no need to loosen in order to be able to open his shirt collar, was equally commonplace.

Why did Calmar feel like a little boy in his presence? And why, when the silences were too long, did he feel obliged to speak, whereas his companion appeared not to mind long pauses and didn't even pretend to doze?

"My father-in-law decided to open a sort of rural restaurant on the way out of Poissy, on a hill overlooking the Seine. You can't really call it a farm, the animals are just part of the setup: two cows, an old horse, a goat, three sheep, a few geese, a few ducks, and some chickens. The guests eat in the main room, under the exposed beams. They love it."

"You go there every Sunday?"

"As a rule, yes. My wife is very attached to her parents. The children are mad about animals and my daughter spends her afternoons riding the horse around the meadow."

He almost expected to hear the question:

"How about you?"

He nearly always went to sleep, fully dressed, in the first room he came to.

At last a little station at which the train did not stop: Sommacampagna. Then came Castelnovo del Garda, Peschiera del Garda, Desenzano, Lonato . . .

"I won't be able to get off at Lausanne as I hoped because I have a plane to catch in Geneva and this train gets me there just in time."

So! For the first time he had spoken about himself. But he still didn't explain why he had taken such a slow train, which stopped at the smallest stations, or why he appeared to have no baggage. If he came from Belgrade or Trieste, there must have been plenty of other trains to Geneva.

"Do you work in a big firm?"

The man was questioning again.

"It's what one would call an expanding concern. It started in an ironmonger's store in Neuilly, then expanded to a workshop in Nanterre. We now have a factory between Dreux and Chartres, and another one is being built in Finistère."

Brescia. People getting off, more than double the number getting on and squeezing ever more tightly into the corridors.

When they got to Milan, Calmar's shirt was soaking. He was hungry.

"I must have time to . . ." he began.

"I don't advise you to leave the carriage. It'll be unhitched and hitched onto another train."

It was true. He hardly had time to grab a sandwich and a bottle of beer through the window. A miniature steam engine pulled them out of the station and left them under the sun in the middle of a network of rails.

"We'll be going back to the station soon."

"Have you taken this train before?"

"I know it. I know nearly all the trains. Our fellow passengers will be getting on in Milan."

He pointed to the reservation slips.

"Two to Lausanne and one to Geneva. The fourth is getting out at Sion."

Yet he hadn't left his seat, not even to go to the toilet. Apart from them, the carriage was almost empty. There were only two American women in the next compartment and a fat man asleep three compartments farther on. Nobody was standing. The two American women were worried. They thought they had been left behind and cast glances of distress at the rails and the station in the distance.

It was hotter than when the train had been moving.

"I suppose you'll be taking the 8:37 to Paris from Lausanne."

Right. He was always right. He knew everything.

"We'll get to Lausanne at 5:05. I wonder if I could

ask you a favor. Unless, of course, you've already made other arrangements."

"Not at all. I don't know what to do in those three hours."

"You know the town?"

"No."

"You don't intend to visit it?"

"Not in this heat."

"On platform one, near the left-baggage office, are some rows of lockers."

He took a key out of his pocket.

"This is the key to number 155. The locker contains a case, neither heavy nor large. But I really think I'm inconveniencing you. . . ."

"Not at all. Go ahead. . . ."

"It means taking out the case, and in order to do so you'll have to put about one and a half Swiss francs into the slot. Here's some change."

Calmar pretended to protest.

"Just a minute! If the train stops long enough in the station, I could do it myself. But the case must then be taken to this address."

He wrote an address on the page of a red notebook, tore it out, and gave it, together with the key, to Calmar.

"It's less than five minutes' taxi ride from the station. Allow me to give you the Swiss money for the taxi."

A jolt. They had been hitched onto a train that was shunting them to another platform, where a row of passengers stood waiting.

"And thanks."

The waiter of the dining car came by, distributing tickets. The stranger took one for the first sitting. Calmar did not have the courage to go and eat. The sandwich and the beer weighed on his stomach. He felt repulsive in his wet shirt, so he contented himself with a little bottle of Campari soda from the trolley.

The passengers to Geneva were English; they had some difficulty fitting their golf bags on the rack. The lady was getting out at Brig and the gentleman, who was reading the *Tribune de Lausanne,* was presumably going to Lausanne.

Calmar remained alone for almost an hour; everybody had followed the bell to the dining car.

They reached Lago Maggiore; in the little station, the rush began again, people crowding into the corridor.

He vaguely heard a shout on the platform:

"Arona! Arona!"

Then Stresa, where he opened his eyes and saw some red roofs under the palm trees. Baveno. Verbania Pallanza...

In Domodossola the corridors were deserted at last and the food carts rushed toward the carriages.

"Passports..."

The passport inspector merely glanced at Calmar's passport and at those of the English couple. He was more attentive with the stranger's, but there was no particular distrust in his eyes when he looked at him after examining his photograph. He stamped the passport, then turned the pages, and handed it back—but with a certain respect, sketching a salute with his hand.

Calmar had been asleep for almost an hour when the sun shone on his face and he awoke, disgruntled, with a nasty taste in his mouth. He bought another bottle of the pink soda, which he had tried that day for the first time.

"Customs! Anything to declare?"

Carabinieri on the platform.

"What's in this suitcase?"

"Clothes, underwear."

Everything appeared to be over but the train waited another fifteen minutes before moving slowly toward the Simplon, and if one looked out one could see the black entrance of the tunnel. Just at that moment Calmar was standing by the door. The lights were on. He felt, more than he saw, his companion get up and go down the corridor. Once the train was in the tunnel Calmar sat down opposite the empty seat, closed the window, and waited.

He didn't like tunnels. On the way to Venice, this one had seemed interminable to him, despite the excitement of his children. After a good ten minutes he was surprised to see no sign of the man who had been sitting opposite him since eight o'clock that morning.

Why did Calmar now get up and go toward the toilet? He expected to see the word "occupied" on the little enamel plaque, but he saw "vacant" and automatically went in to wash his hands.

The man had still not returned to the compartment. Nor was he there when the train came out into the sunlight and stopped at the Swiss station of Brig, where other passport inspectors and customs officers got on.

"Passports."

"Anything to declare?"

"Clothes, underwear. I'm on my way to Paris."

The officer looked at the empty seat and the reservation slip.

"Isn't anyone sitting there?"

"There *was* somebody. He left the compartment as we were going into the tunnel."

"How about his baggage?"

"He didn't have any. Unless . . ."

"Unless what?"

"Unless it's in the baggage car."

The man wrote something in his notebook.

"Thank you."

That was all. The lady had got off. Some passengers were buying chocolate. The train moved on again, its corridors empty, along the Rhone. The white water looked marvelously cool.

Two more stops, no rush, no crowd, no farewells: Sion, then, on the Lake of Geneva, Montreaux.

The man had still not reappeared when the train reached Lausanne, and Calmar had searched it from end to end.

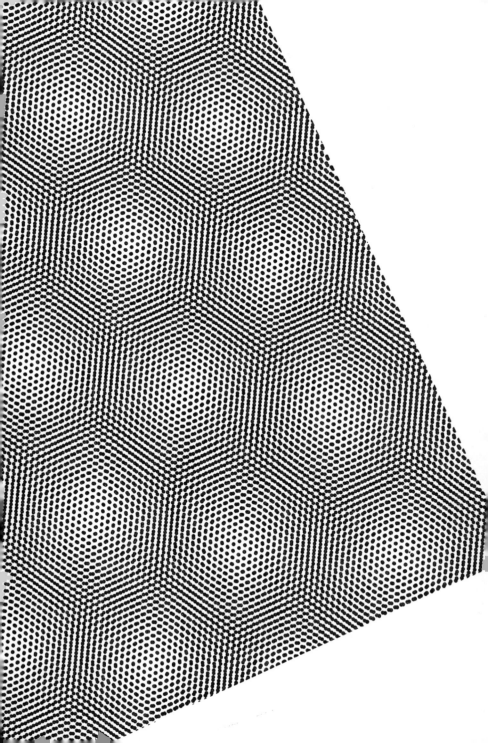

So far he had spent the day like any other day of travel, dazed by the sun, the heat, the blue curtain flapping obsessively. He was not aware that he was taking anything in, and it was only later, searching in the jumble of impressions and images of barely coherent thoughts that he discovered any precise memories.

After Lausanne, on the other hand, everything became perfectly clear, in him and around him. Everything impressed itself on his memory with the precision of a daguerreotype. It was as though he had suddenly become two people, one watching the other; as though he were observing lucidly the somewhat portly Justin Calmar, short in the leg, brown hair glued to his forehead with sweat, standing motionless and undecided at first, on platform five, his two suitcases next to him.

And from that moment on he was faced with choices, a succession of decisions to make, which he wanted to ponder honestly (since he had always been honest), energetically, perhaps even a little complacently.

In the confusion of the departure from Venice, he especially remembered his daughter in a red bathing suit, an ice-cream cone in her hand. He had also been vaguely aware of a man in his compartment looking him up and down, and a little later he had noticed that this man was holding a newspaper printed in some Slavic language.

Little by little, by dint of asking one harmless question after another, the man had obtained a quantity of information about his life, his family, and his job, which he had supplied with a docility that made him feel slightly ashamed.

Why had the stranger appeared so exceptional to

him? There was nothing especially striking about his appearance except for his serenity, his eyes, which seemed to be looking at nothing but which noticed everything.

Maybe Calmar had said to himself, He must be tough!

Just as his boss was tough. Joseph Baudelin, a former ironmonger on Avenue de Neuilly who had become an important industrialist. And even though Calmar did not consider himself a weakling, he had a vague admiration for people who were tough, who didn't need anyone else, who required no rules, who didn't smile when they were spoken to, who remained themselves at all times, without caring what others thought of them.

Did his boss need to tell himself that he was honest, for instance? Was his fellow passenger honest, did he try to appear so?

The first problem was whether Calmar should report his disappearance to anyone, to the stationmaster or to a police inspector.

But, after all, Calmar had already mentioned it once, however vaguely, to the customs officer at Brig.

What was there to prevent the man from entering another compartment, from getting out at Brig and leaving the station, lost in the crowd?

Anyhow, what business was it of Calmar's? He had been given a mission to perform. The term was too strong. A mere errand, which anyone could have carried out just as well as he. In his pocket he had the key of a baggage locker, some Swiss coins, and a ten-franc note for the taxi.

He went down into the underpass, where, as at Brig, chocolate was on sale, and he came out at platform one. He had plenty of time. First he went to the left-baggage office, where he had to stand in line for several minutes before checking his two suitcases.

The metal lockers were opposite, each with a number

on it, and when he found number 155, he noticed that there was only one and a half francs to pay.

He still knew nothing, foresaw nothing. Nevertheless, there was something furtive in his gestures, in the way he looked over his shoulder, as if he were performing not so much a reprehensible action as an equivocal one.

It was not he who had put the case in the locker. From reading the instructions he discovered that the rate was thirty centimes a day, in other words the case had been left five days earlier.

In what circumstances, and when, had the key found its way into the hands of the stranger who had been in Trieste or in Belgrade as recently as last night?

As he slipped the key into the lock he felt that a sort of complicity had arisen between himself and the stranger. But complicity in what?

He put a one-franc piece and then a fifty-centime piece into the slot, turned the key, and, making sure that no one was looking, took hold of a brown case, neither heavy nor large.

It was more like what businessmen call an attaché case, five inches thick, eighteen inches long, and twelve inches wide.

A few minutes later he had left the station and taken the first taxi parked outside. Some strapping big fellows were walking by in shorts and hobnailed shoes, green knapsacks on their backs, little green caps on their heads, as on postcards, and a strong smell of male sweat and mess kits struck his nostrils, as though he were watching soldiers returning from parade.

He took from his wallet the slip of paper the man had given him and which he had not yet bothered to look at: Arlette Staub, 24 Rue du Bugnon.

"Twenty-four Rue du Bugnon. I've been told it's only a five minutes' drive."

"Not even that. Not on Sundays."

He had forgotten it was Sunday, and if the main

roads were crowded with cars the city streets were silent and almost deserted.

The taxi climbed, turned, climbed again: the whole of Lausanne seemed to be built on a steep slope. He noticed some enormous buildings, the district hospital with invalids and nurses at every window and on every balcony.

He didn't realize that the car had stopped.

"Here it is."

A row of modern buildings opposite the hospital with a balcony for every apartment. The taxi had stopped in front of a bar with a pale-green awning over some tables.

"Wait for me. I won't be more than a couple of minutes."

The driver didn't even bother to answer. Calmar began to feel slightly guilty. But once again, he was not doing anything reprehensible, forbidden, by taking this case to an address a stranger had scribbled on a piece of paper. So why did he prefer to pass unnoticed, and why did he wonder whether the people drinking coffee and beer in the café were struck by his off-white suit with its Italian cut?

He expected to find a concierge, as in Paris. Instead, he saw a row of mailboxes with a visiting card or a name written in ink on each one. There were four rows of them, undoubtedly corresponding to the floor, and Arlette Staub's name was followed by the number 37 in the third row.

He took the elevator up to a long hallway. Again on every door there was a visiting card or a name written by hand. On each door, too, there was a glass circle, the size of a button, through which the tenants could see their visitors before opening.

Thirty-seven . . . the last door at the end of the hall-way. He pressed the electric bell, suddenly sweating profusely, as though it were the hottest moment of the day, eager to get it over with, overcome with panic for no apparent reason.

Was he being watched through that glass eye in the mahogany or rosewood door?

He rang again, impatiently, listened, and, since the door still didn't move and he heard no sound inside the apartment, unthinkingly he put his hand on the knob.

The door gave way almost without his pushing it and he stepped forward.

"Is anyone at home? . . . Mademoiselle Staub! . . . Is anyone at home? . . ."

A beige linen coat was hanging in the hall and, to the left, an open door led to a sunlit living room. The door onto the balcony was also wide open and the breeze from outside swelled the curtains as on the train from Venice.

"Hello! . . . Is anyone in?"

He added stupidly:

"Isn't anyone in?"

He was tempted to put the case on the floor and leave, shutting the door behind him, and to drive back to the station. He was just about to do so when, at the foot of a pale-blue couch, he saw a pair of shoes, two legs, a petticoat, and then, finally, the neck and reddish hair of a woman. She was lying full length on a carpet of a darker blue than the couch, one arm stretched out, the other folded behind her back, as though it had been twisted.

He did not see her face because she was lying on her stomach. He didn't see any blood, either. He leaned over and touched her hand.

"Mademoiselle Staub!"

But it was obvious that Mademoiselle Staub was dead. He didn't stop to think or to ponder the various possible ways of behaving. He went out, backward, slammed the door, and, without bothering to call the elevator, ran down the stairs. It was only downstairs that he realized he was still holding the attaché case.

For a split second he thought of going up again, but the driver had seen him and, leaning out of the taxi, was opening the door for him.

Luckily! Otherwise he might have gone into the little café and ordered a drink to pull himself together.

"To the station?"

"Yes, to the station."

There or anywhere else. He was in a hurry to get away. While the taxi wound its way down the street he looked out at the block and saw a couple leaning over a balcony, a child, in a red bathing suit like his daughter's, playing on another, squatting in front of a brightly colored go-cart. On the fourth floor he thought he could see a woman sunbathing, also lying on her stomach.

What should he have done? He thought he had seen a telephone in the living room on the third floor. Shouldn't he have called the police immediately? It hadn't even occurred to him. His sole concern had been to get away from the dead woman as quickly as possible, and only now was he aware of what had happened.

What could he have told the policemen who found him in a strange apartment by the body of a woman he had never met in a town in which he had set foot today for the first time in his life?

"I was told to give her this case. . . ."

"By whom?"

"I don't know. An elderly man in the same compartment as myself in the train from Venice."

"His name? His address?"

"I don't know."

"Why did he ask you to do it?"

"Because he had to go on to Geneva and the train

only stopped for three or four minutes at the station."

"There are other trains."

"He had a plane to catch at Cointrin."

"Where to?"

"He didn't tell me."

"But he gave you the case, telling you that he was going to catch a plane?"

"Yes."

"So he's on his way to Geneva at the moment?"

"I don't think so."

"Why not?"

"Because I didn't see him in the train after the Simplon tunnel."

"So you think he got off the train in the middle of the tunnel?"

"I don't know."

"Yet you came here with the case. Where did he give it to you?"

"He didn't give it to me in person. He gave me the key to a locker in the station . . . number 155 . . . I can remember the number. He also gave me some Swiss coins and a ten-franc note for the taxi. . . ."

It was impossible! He visualized the scene, the same questions at the police station, and then again in the offices of the district attorney.

He hadn't done anything wrong. He hadn't even intended to do anyone a favor. You could almost say that he had been forced to do as he did, that the case had come into his hands by a concurrence of fortuitous circumstances, and that he had not opened Arlette Staub's door of his own free will. A few minutes earlier he had not even known her name, although it was written on a slip of paper in his wallet.

She looked dead. Her hand was stone cold. He had no idea how she had died. All he knew was that she was wearing high-heeled shoes, stockings, a pale-pink silk petticoat, and that she looked like a woman who, when death struck, in whatever manner, was in the process of getting dressed.

She had still to put on her dress and pick up her handbag, which was on the couch.

The living room was smart, luxurious. There must have been a bathroom, a kitchen, perhaps even another room? Unless the couch became a bed at night. He didn't know. He was making conjectures. Once again he knew nothing.

But he couldn't tell people he knew nothing.

"Four francs seventy . . ."

He handed the driver the ten-franc note and wondered whether or not to leave the attaché case in the taxi. But another passenger might find it after he had left for Paris and, with his cream-colored suit crumpled by the hours spent on the train from Venice, he was really too conspicuous.

It was only half past six. Back there, at the Lido, Dominique and the children had left the beach, where it usually grew cool in the evening, to take their bathrobes, buckets and spades, the balloon, and the large canvas bag back to the boardinghouse.

"Can't I have my shower tomorrow morning, Ma . . . Look, I'm not dirty."

The same old story every evening.

"You're both covered with sand."

"Sand isn't dirty . . . the sea water cleans everything. . . ."

"Don't argue, children. You're going to give me another headache. . . ."

Generally Dominique would call:

"Justin! You tell them. If only your daughter didn't always have to argue . . ."

He went to the station washroom, vaguely intending to leave the case behind, but he realized that this would not pass unnoticed. He came out disheartened. He almost wanted to sit on one of the steps and stay there, waiting for something to happen, his head in his hands.

Two more hours to wait, the most dangerous hours, it seemed to him.

Whether rightly or wrongly, he thought that he would feel better on the train, once he had crossed the border.

He opened the door of the first-class restaurant. He didn't see a bar so he sat down and ordered a whisky, something he very seldom did, for he hardly ever drank anything other than a little wine at meals. It was the stranger who had given him a taste for Campari soda, and he had drunk five or six small bottles in the course of the day.

"I'm an honest man!"

He always had been. He had always done his best. He had often made sacrifices for other people, as he had done this time, spending his holidays on a beach he had hated from the first moment.

The rooms in the boardinghouse were tiny and they had no washing facilities. He sometimes had to wait half an hour for the shower room at the end of the hall to be free. The children wanted the door between their room and their parents' to be kept open, so that, for two weeks, his wife and he had only been able to snatch a few minutes' intimacy, interrupted by Dominique's exclamations: "Sh . . ." or "Be careful!"

Did he deserve to be in this position, to feel guilty as though he were a criminal, and to behave like a criminal?

Why had the man whose name he didn't know disappeared between Domodossola and Brig, while the train was going through the interminable Simplon tunnel? He hadn't given the impression, throughout the day, of a man about to commit suicide.

Nevertheless, on a mere pretext—for it looked more and more like a pretext—he had sent Calmar, whom he had never set eyes on before, on an errand that must have been important.

And what did that case, now standing on a chair next to him, contain?

And if the man had not committed suicide, why and how had he disappeared? Had somebody pushed him out of the train as he was going into or coming out of the toilet?

This was almost more likely than his vanishing at Brig, lost in the crowd, because it was a frontier post and everybody's passport was examined both on the train and on the way out of the station.

"Miss . . ."

He clicked his fingers to attract the waitress's attention.

"The same again, please."

"One whisky, one . . ."

And what if the French customs officers told him to open the case—as they would very probably do—to which he didn't even have the key?

"I'm sorry, gentlemen . . . I lost the key. . . ."

Well, this case was solid enough, made of genuine, thick leather and not plastic—and he ought to know, after having worked in the plastics industry for almost ten years!

It was battered, of course. It wasn't much to look at. It must have been carted around plenty of offices, plenty of station and airport waiting rooms, to be so battered, but the locks were of excellent quality: they were not the cheap locks you can pick with a penknife.

"Dear God, please . . ."

He didn't believe in God, or he no longer believed in him. Or perhaps he did believe a little, at heart, when things got rough. When Josée had had to have an operation for acute appendicitis two years earlier he had also murmured:

"Dear God, please . . ."

He had even made some vow, but he could no longer remember what it was, and besides, he hadn't kept it. What would his daughter or his wife think when they were told that he had been arrested as a suspect for the murder of a young woman in a strange apartment in Lausanne?

And how about Monsieur Baudelin? And his friend Bob, the designer, and all his colleagues?

"I might have something to eat. Is there a dining car on the train to Paris?"

"The 8:37? I'm afraid not. What may I bring you? There's fillet of perch, creamed chicken, and pigeon pie."

He wasn't hungry, but he ordered a pigeon pie because of the name and because he hardly ever ate pigeon at home.

"What would you like to drink? Swiss wine or Beaujolais?"

"Beaujolais . . ."

He didn't care. He didn't care about anything except the case that had fastened itself to him and the suit that his wife had insisted he wear and that made him as conspicuous as if he had been waving a flag.

"Dear God, please . . ."

There were five other passengers, including a priest, in the compartment, and Calmar didn't even have a corner seat. He sat between a lady in her fifties who was constantly drawing away from him, as though physical contact with him bothered her, and an old man, with the rosette of the Legion of Honor, who was reading the *Figaro* until he fell asleep, once they had passed the French frontier, as peaceably as if he had been in his own bed.

The priest sitting opposite him wore black shoes with large silver buckles. Facing the lady, her husband, a small, thin, nervous man, apologized profusely every time he sneaked past the other passengers' legs to go to the toilet at the end of the corridor.

"Did you take your pills?"

"Yes. Immediately after dinner in Lausanne."

"Two of them?"

"Yes, of course."

"Have you got indigestion?"

He looked at the others in embarrassment, hoping they hadn't heard.

"You shouldn't have eaten calf's tongue. You know it doesn't agree with you."

A girl sitting by herself in the other corner, tall and slim, exposed her legs candidly. She had reddish hair, like Arlette Staub, and every time Calmar caught an involuntary glimpse of the flesh above her stockings he thought of the body on the blue carpet in the apartment on Rue du Bugnon.

The most surprising part of it all was that, if he had met Arlette anywhere, in the train for example, he wouldn't have recognized her. He must find out. The French papers were unlikely to mention her death unless it was a sensational crime.

The local paper seemed to be the *Gazette de Lausanne*. He had once been told that the newspaper booth in Place de l'Opéra, opposite the Café de la Paix, sold papers from every country, and he resolved to go and buy the Swiss paper the next morning.

Would there be a report on the incident already? Would the body have been discovered by now? If the young woman lived on her own, if she had no maid, it would be some days, especially in the holiday period, before anyone took any notice of her.

He shouldn't have had whisky or eaten pigeon pie. He felt as ill as his neighbor's husband and, had he been able to, would have vomited in the toilet. The approach of the frontier made him feel sick. He had never felt so lonely in his life, and this was a feeling he hated more than anything else.

If he really had been alone in the compartment, he might have suffered less. But there were six people looking at each other, with no contact between them, and all the glances, not only the ones in his direction but also those directed at the others, seemed suspicious or accusatory.

Even the woman on his left and her husband. She was cross with him for having eaten what he had eaten, for bothering the others every time he got up, and he was angry with her for her lack of understanding and her reproaches.

Calmar never felt altogether happy in a crowd, and if the purchase of a motor car had seemed such a deliverance to him it was not because it enabled him to drive wherever he wanted, but because it spared him the scrutiny people give each other in the subway or on the bus.

He would never admit it to Dominique, of course, but he had married primarily in order not to be alone. He loved her, of course. He had found her attractive the moment they first met. Yet if he had never met her he would have married someone else.

And, just as his neighbor resented her husband, so he resented Dominique for having forced the crowd of the Lido on him, above all for having forced him into the promiscuity of the boardinghouse, where the guests scrutinized each other in the dining room as they would have done in the dining car of a train.

Worse still, he even resented her looking at him. He resented her looking at him as though she were thinking:

Who is this man, after all? He is my husband. I've been living with him for thirteen years. We sleep in the same bed. Our bodies have no secrets. But when he comes back from the office and kisses me, what goes on in his mind? What has he been doing? What would happen if I died? What does he really feel about his children?

The train had already arrived at Vallorbe and there was the usual to-do of passport inspectors and customs officers.

"Have your passports ready, please. . . ."

He expected guiltily that his would be examined more closely than the others, but the inspector returned it to him with no more than a vague glance.

"Anything to declare?"

Even the priest's expression had changed. Like the others, he looked falsely innocent.

"Nothing . . ."

"What's in this suitcase?"

"Clothes, underwear, a few devotional objects I'm bringing back from Rome for my parishioners . . ."

"No gold, jewels or watches? No chocolates, cigars, cigarettes?"

The husband of the lady was obliged to climb onto the seat and pull down the brown suitcase, which he was asked to open, and the customs officer slipped his hands under the clothes and linen.

"What's in this case?"

"Business papers," said Calmar with a naturalness that surprised him.

"Is this suitcase yours?"

"Yes."

"Open it. . . ."

Ah! He had nothing to declare in the suitcase and the customs officer gave him absolution and went on to the next compartment without having punished any of them.

Other passengers must have had a dirtier conscience,

because a couple laden with heavy suitcases were taken off to the customs office and the woman, perched on her high heels, walked like somebody expecting trouble.

The train moved off again, with its silent sleeping cars, which Calmar had not had time to book, and with its ordinary cars, like this one, where the light was turned low and the passengers tried to sleep. Only the old gentleman snored softly, while the girl sitting opposite him curled up like a gun dog and exposed still more of her legs.

He tried not to think; he tried to yield to the motion of the train, but as soon as he thought he was dropping off to sleep some detail of the day came back to him and his mind set to work again.

Why had the stranger picked him in Venice?

It was idiotic. He hadn't picked him, since there was nobody else in the compartment. Nevertheless, he had put him through a sort of exam. His questions were not gratuitous. He wanted to know what sort of man he was dealing with.

And he knew at once. An honest man. An idiotically honest man on whom he could rely to perform an errand such as this.

Otherwise he would undoubtedly have changed compartments and applied to someone else.

As for his disappearing . . . for a second he thought he had been kidnaped, but one can't remove someone from a train in a tunnel like the Simplon!

So it was either a voluntary disappearance or suicide. In either case he had been deceived, somehow or other.

Of course, the man had no idea that Arlette Staub was dead. Otherwise he wouldn't have taken such pains to get the case to her. After all, she no longer needed it.

In short, Calmar was wrong to be so severe; if the

young woman had not been dead his part would have been limited to the banal and innocuous role of a benevolent messenger.

And yet . . . there was the automatic locker where the case had been stored for only five days, and the stranger, who came from beyond Venice—from Trieste or Belgrade, if not from farther away—had the key to it. Had it been sent to him in an express letter? Had he deposited the case before leaving?

But why? Why this? Why that? Why him? Why everything?

He dropped off to sleep at last, vaguely hearing people shouting Dijon, doors banging, orders given by the guards, and when he woke up it was broad daylight. The priest was awake and looking at him, and was embarrassed to catch his eye, as though he had taken advantage of his being asleep to examine him. Examination of conscience . . .

It was idiotic! He must stop thinking like that. He got up, took his razor out of his suitcase and shut himself into the toilet. When he came out he remained in the corridor, tried to make out where he was, recognized the banks of the Seine near Melun, set out in search of the dining car, passing through half a dozen cars before finding a ticket collector who told him there wasn't one. . . .

Finally, at half past six in the morning, the train arrived at Gare de Lyon. He had to walk the length of the train because his car was at the far end. As he passed the newspaper stand he asked:

"Do you get the *Tribune de Lausanne?*"

"The *Tribune* and the *Gazette,* yes sir."

"I suppose you don't have this morning's."

"The Monday paper comes in only about half past twelve."

"Can one get it in town, too?"

"They must surely carry it at the stands on the Champs Élysées and Place de l'Opéra."

"Thank you."

His one obsessive idea was to get home safe and sound. He said to a taxi driver:

"Rue Legendre . . . I'll tell you where to stop. . . ."

But he kept the taxi waiting in front of a small café because he had run out of cigarettes and wanted a cup of coffee. He ate two croissants mechanically. Despite his anxiety they gave him pleasure; he had at last come back to the genuine croissants of Paris.

"Another coffee, please."

His home. His concierge, whom he couldn't avoid.

"And how is Madame Calmar, Monsieur? And the children? I'm sure they can't get enough of the marvels of Venice, the darlings. . . ."

She gave him some printed matter and a few bills that had arrived after she had stopped forwarding his mail.

"You'll find the house very empty. It's already the twentieth of August and hardly anyone is back. The same with the shops. You have no idea how far I have to go to buy the meat!"

The good old elevator, slightly wobbly, but with its familiar and indefinable smell. The stairs covered with brown carpet. The brown door with its brass knob, a little tarnished now that Dominique was not there to polish it every day.

But his first view of the apartment was disappointing. It was all dark. He hadn't thought that the shutters would be closed, and now his first concern was to open them all, even in the children's room. As he passed the refrigerator he decided to plug it in, and it was only then that he came back to the dining room, where he had left the attaché case on the table.

Was he really going to open it, force it open? Theoretically, he had no right to do so; neither the case nor its contents were his.

But, after all that had happened, was it not necessary, indispensable, to know the nature of its contents?

He cheated, knowing full well that it was not a question of duty but of curiosity, a need to know.

And why not a question of self-defense? After all, because of this case he had just spent several hours that normally only a criminal would have experienced. Well, the case would obviously contain the explanation of these mishaps.

He, too, had a case that locked—he used it to carry his work home from the office—and he went to search through his bunch of keys, which he kept in a drawer in the bedroom. His attention was attracted by the alarm clock. It had stopped. He took time out to wind it up, as though he were still hesitant, and then wound up the clock on the marble mantelpiece in the dining room, too. Of course, the key didn't fit and he managed to twist it. It was cheap merchandise.

He went to the kitchen where they kept the tools found in every household: hammer, screwdriver, pliers, pincers, all jumbled together with the corkscrew and various types of bottle openers.

He gave himself a last moment of grace: he went to lock the front door, as though his sense of guilt had increased. Finally, after taking off his jacket and his tie, he tried to force the two locks, first with the pincers, then with the pliers, and at last succeeded in doing so with the screwdriver.

The two metal clasps broke. The lid rose slightly. He had only to lift it with his hand and he found himself confronted by wad upon wad of bank notes, well packed, as if by a cashier.

They weren't French francs. They were mainly hundred-dollar bills, a hundred in each wad, he reckoned at first sight, as well as some fifty-pound notes, and slimmer wads of Swiss francs.

His first reaction was to look over at the building across the street, but the woman who was moving to and fro, busy with housekeeping chores in her bedroom, didn't once turn in his direction.

"Not right away . . ." he murmured to himself.

Not now. He needed to recover, to think things over. He was exhausted, feverish after a day and a night spent on the train. He didn't feel normal. He had to get his balance back.

He took the case with him, slid it, half closed, under the bureau in the bedroom, and a few minutes later, after turning on the bathtub faucets, he undressed.

He had never felt so naked or so lonely in his life.

"When you get back to Paris your suit will have to go to the cleaners. For heaven's sake, don't put it in the laundry hamper. Madame Léonard is quite capable of sending it to the laundry and I don't trust those materials that tend to shrink. You'd better take it yourself to the cleaners on Rue des Dames."

Only twice before had he lived alone in the apartment on Rue Legendre: when Dominique had gone to the hospital to have her children. No, three times; because she had once gone to Le Havre for three days when her sister, the wife of a headwaiter on the Transatlantic Lines, was having a baby.

Was it in protest against this voice he seemed to hear that he stuffed the cream-colored suit into the laundry hamper?

"You'll be dead tired when you get home, darling. Since you've only got to be in the office in the afternoon, do try and get some sleep, and let Madame Léonard unpack for you."

Madame Léonard was the maid who came two afternoons a week. She was a tiny, wizened little woman but with a disproportionately large behind thrust out in a way that made her look as though she were constantly rushing forward. For a long time she had been married to an invalid, whom she had looked after for almost twenty years. She did housework all day long, and at night often went to dress the corpses in the district.

She lived alone in a garret in a nearby street, never talking to anybody and simply muttering:

"Those rich, they're all crazy!"

As far as she was concerned, the rich were her employers, the tradesmen, and even the concierge.

3

He thought about her as he lay in the bathtub, wondering how she could live like that without ever giving in to despair. Weren't there thousands, tens of thousands of people like her in Paris, not to mention the even more unfortunate ones barely able to move across their rooms or immobilized in their beds, depending on the mercy of their neighbors or some social worker?

There was a fortune under the bureau. He didn't know how much and he didn't want to know, yet.

"Try and sleep and ..."

He tried, because he really was tired. He put his pajamas on, as though he were not alone, and, after drawing the curtains, lay down on the bed. Whatever he did, the attaché case was on his mind and he asked himself questions about it—somewhat confused questions because, after twenty-four hours on the train, the bath had made him drowsy.

Was the stranger on the train from Venice an international thief who had used him deliberately in order not to run the risk of picking up the case himself?

In that case, why had Arlette Staub been killed? That reminded him: he had kept the slip of paper on which her address was scribbled in his wallet. That was dangerous. The slip might drop out of his wallet in the office just as he was taking it out of his pocket. And what if the name were in the papers ...

He got up, went to the bureau where he had put the contents of his pockets, and tore the slip of paper into tiny pieces. He was going to throw them into the wastepaper basket when it occurred to him that Madame Léonard, who would be alone in the apartment that afternoon, might be curious enough to reconstruct the puzzle.

He suddenly became maniacally prudent. He burned the pieces of paper in an ash tray, threw the ashes into the toilet and flushed.

When he lay down again he was no longer sleepy. He didn't try to close his eyes. And what if the money was counterfeit? He could see the stranger on the train at the head of an organization of counterfeiters. Anything was possible. Gunrunning? Espionage?

How much money was there in the case? As if to prove to himself how calm he was, he had resolved not to count it until later, toward the end of the morning, after two or three hours' rest. But he got up again, leaving the curtains drawn just in case, because of the woman opposite, and sat down at Dominique's dressing table.

There were a hundred notes in each wad of dollars, which meant that the wads, slimmer than a paperback, must have been worth ten thousand dollars.

Twenty wads. These notes that looked so new were worth two hundred thousand dollars in all! As for the English bank notes, he counted fifty packets each with fifty twenty-pound notes, in other words fifty thousand pounds.

He went to get a piece of paper and a pencil and worked out the total amount contained in the attaché case. The dollars were worth about a million new francs. He felt quite giddy. He was sweating from every pore and his hand started trembling.

A million francs! Plus almost seven hundred thousand francs in English pounds! And that did not include some loose bills at the bottom of the case that no one had bothered to bundle with an elastic band like the others: twenty thousand German marks and ten notes of one thousand Swiss francs each, wide and thick.

"I've come to bring you an attaché case, Inspector. Someone on the Venice train gave me a key and asked me to . . . He had written an address on a piece of paper . . . I burned it just now . . . Why? Because of

Madame Léonard, the maid . . . No, I didn't intend to keep the money. If I forced the lock . . ."

It was inconceivable. Nobody in his right mind would believe his story.

"I took a taxi to the address on the slip, to Rue du Bugnon, to the apartment of someone named Arlette Staub. I rang the bell. Since no one answered, I automatically turned the doorknob and the door opened. . . . The young woman was dead . . . I presume she had been murdered. I didn't see any blood . . . perhaps she'd been strangled? . . . The Lausanne police must know about it by now. . . ."

He was still more worried when he suddenly realized that he would have to hide the case, or at least its contents. He could throw the case away, into the Seine, for example, as soon as it was dark, and he could lock it into one of the drawers for the afternoon.

Would Madame Léonard notice that the drawers were locked? For he would have to lock all three of them, something he had never done before.

For the first time, he realized that no piece of furniture in the apartment had ever been locked, that there was no place at all to hide any object.

His wife, his children, Madame Léonard, anybody visiting, his sister-in-law or his mother-in-law, might open any drawer or any closet.

And on Saturday his wife and children would come back from their vacation. He hadn't made any decision yet. If he was looking for a hiding place, it wasn't because he intended to keep the money. For good, that is. But he still had to wait a little, to make further inquiries.

Slowly, still in his pajamas, he went through all the rooms. First around their bedroom, the room of an average couple, with fairly modern furniture of fairly good quality, but utterly nondescript. There must have been rooms looking exactly like this one in thousands of other more or less similar apartments.

But even this was a step forward. When they got married they had lived in a two-room apartment in an old building on Boulevard des Batignolles, and they had bought some secondhand furniture. They had bought, in particular, a very high walnut bed, like the ones he had seen in his parents' room throughout his childhood.

Their present bed was low and it had taken him a long time to get used to it. Also to get used to the lightness of the bureau and of the two armchairs, covered in orange velvet, of the dining-room table and the dressing table.

It was his in-laws' apartment that he had inherited when Louis Lavaud, his wife's father, had retired from his job as headwaiter at Wepler's on Place Clichy in order to run his own establishment on the hill of Poissy.

When the Lavauds had lived there the apartment had been dark. The present living room, as contemporary now as the bedroom, had been papered with bronzed imitation Cordovan leather.

"You can do as you please, children, because this is your apartment now, but you won't find another wallpaper of this quality. You can wash it down without raising a single blister. How many times have you washed it, Joséphine?"

In those days, too, the furniture had been heavy, made of massive wood, and the chairs around the main table had been covered with embossed leather.

Just like his parents' house in Gien! Except that there the dining room was hardly ever used; the meals were eaten in the kitchen, behind the shop.

He wasn't a thief. He didn't intend to use this money, which, for the time being, didn't seem to belong to anybody.

Supposing he gave the police a description of the stranger in the train . . . supposing they found him alive . . . wouldn't that be to betray his trust?

And he had not trusted him purely by chance. After all, they had been traveling in the same compartment. The man had observed him at length, had asked him precise questions, such precise questions that, by the time they got to Milan, he knew nearly all there was to know about his life.

He even knew that when he was in elementary school, and later, at the lycée, his schoolfellows had called him the "Maggot." Not only because he was chubbier than the others. He got the nickname because his father sold fishing tackle at Quai Lenoir, not far from the old bridge across the Loire.

The house was narrow and high with a fretwork gable, like the ones one can still see in Brussels. The shop, too, was narrow, cluttered with reed or bamboo rods, surrounded by glass-fronted drawers containing floats of every color and size, silk and horsehair lines, rolls of catgut, leads, hundreds, maybe thousands of articles, which only his father knew how to find.

In addition to everything else, he sold maggots and worms, and on Sundays he always had a container full of gudgeon for pike fishing.

His father was tall and thin, the very opposite of himself, with fair hair and a light, drooping mustache, and Justin had given him a nickname he had never told anyone about: the "anemic Gaul."

For his skin was pale, with reddish blotches, and he always looked tired, as though his long body were going to break in two.

He died young, aged forty-two, of a lung infection. His mother said it was pneumonia, but it was more likely to have been tuberculosis.

She had continued to run the business. She still owned it, and ran it with old Oscar, who went to fish for gudgeon every Saturday evening with a casting net and who kept the "maggot factory" at the bottom of the little garden. Because of the neighbors' complaints, they had built an arbor to camouflage the pole on which they had stuck a sheepshead provided by the butcher. After a few days the maggots got into it and dropped into a sieve lined with sawdust.

They were sold by the spoonful. When Calmar was a child a soupspoonful of maggots cost twenty-five centimes.

Why did he think of all these things as he looked for a place to hide the bank notes? But there was no hiding place. There was nowhere to hide any more. When they had just got married, though, they still had an enormous wardrobe with a mirror; it was just possible to hide an object behind the cornice on top of it.

He went to get his own briefcase, emptied it—it contained only printed matter—and stuffed the notes into it. He pulled out a hundred-dollar bill, just one, with which he was going to make an experiment.

It was a necessary experiment. He had nothing—he would never have anything—of the thief about him. But shouldn't he know, in order to regulate his behavior, whether the money was genuine or forged?

"Have all your meals at Étienne's, Justin. . . ."

A mania, one of the manias you encounter in every married couple. Or perhaps it might better be called a tradition. When he was still teaching at the Lycée Carnot and they had very little money, they would occasionally treat themselves to a real meal at a restaurant on Boulevard des Batignolles, an old-fashioned restaurant with mirrors on the walls, a high desk for the cashier, and metal knobs for the dishcloths. The cashier was Madame Étienne. Monsieur Étienne, who had a large red nose, went from one client to another, recommending Normandy sole or stew.

They had gone there quite frequently when Dominique was pregnant. They had also dined there on the occasion of several marriage anniversaries.

And his wife still believed that the only place where you could get good, wholesome food was Étienne's.

Well, he wouldn't be lunching at Étienne's. He had other things to do, other worries. And to call them worries was putting it mildly!

He dressed after opening the curtains. He switched the radio on but all he heard were songs and advertisements.

"The number of special trains this weekend has beaten every record, since most people on a vacation trip have taken an extra day off for the August bank holiday. . . ."

It was unlikely that Radio Europe or Radio-Luxembourg would mention a young woman found dead in an apartment in Lausanne, unless she were connected with some important international racket. And it would be almost impossible for anybody to know that if they didn't know about the existence of the attaché case.

At the newspaper booth in the station he had been told that the Lausanne newspapers would arrive at about twelve or half past twelve.

He couldn't leave the case with its two broken locks in the apartment, at the mercy of Madame Léonard's curiosity. He preferred to wrap it up. There again he realized the difficulty of doing certain things that seem perfectly natural at first sight. There was no wrapping paper in the house!

One drawer contained plenty of pieces of string— the drawer with the tools and bottle openers—but nowhere could he find that thick brown paper used for wrapping parcels.

Because of the vacation and the housecleaning done by Madame Léonard in their absence, there were no old newspapers, either.

He remembered that there were sheets of paper, not brown but blue, lining the bureau drawers. He took out a sheet, which he would have plenty of time to replace. It would look newer than the others. Dominique might notice it.

"Say! You changed the paper in the second drawer?"

The drawer with his shirts and underclothes. What could he reply?

"I spilled . . ."

Spilled what? One doesn't drink a cup of coffee or a glass of wine while choosing a shirt from a drawer.

"I dropped my cigarette and . . ."

He would think of something. If he let himself be obsessed by these details, he would never find a solution.

He wrapped as firm a parcel as he could, locked his own briefcase, and put it in the usual closet, convinced that it would never occur to Madame Léonard to force a lock, as he had done.

He was thinking too much. He must keep calm. Think things over by all means before taking a decision, but think them over without undue anxiety.

He went downstairs. The concierge greeted him.

"I thought you were . . . after such a tiring journey . . ."

"Unfortunately, I have things to do, Madame Godeau."

"Take care of yourself. I'm sure that Madame Calmar wouldn't want you badly taken care of when she's away. If I think of my own poor husband . . . I left him only for a fortnight all the years we lived together, and I know what happens to men once they're on their own. . . ."

A little farther down the street he went into the garage where he had left his car.

"Ah! Monsieur Calmar . . . I thought you weren't

coming back until next week. I must have got the date wrong . . . it won't take long."

Still, they had to move ten other cars before getting to his, which was at the far end of the garage covered with dust.

"I'm sorry about that. If only I'd known . . . just let me pass a rag over it."

His parcel embarrassed him. He hoped the garage owner wouldn't notice it. Instead of putting it in the trunk, he decided to throw it negligently onto the seat.

"A fine day, despite the heat. I don't know what sort of weather you had, but here it hasn't been so hot for years. You know the neighborhood as well as I do, you've been living here for thirteen years . . . they're decent people. Well, I saw housewives do their shopping in shorts, as though they were on the beach, and children playing in the streets in bathing suits. . . ."

He drove toward the Opéra through almost deserted streets. On Rue Auber he even found room to park his car and he hurried to a bank on one of the boulevards.

As he ran up the steps and walked into the hall, cool and dark after the heat outside, he felt panic-stricken.

He realized that this was the first important step. No! The first step had been to open the locker on platform one in the Lausanne station . . . not really, because at that moment the stranger's story was still plausible. Might it be ultimately possible, by moving heaven and earth, to find the Italian ticket collector who had clipped the tickets near Padua and who would undoubtedly remember the yellow slip he had torn out of the stranger's bunch of tickets? There was also the passport inspector at Domodossola who had examined his passport slowly and given him an almost respectful salute.

Why had he saluted him? After all, he hadn't saluted Calmar. Was the stranger famous in some way, was he in an important position somewhere? A diplomat, for example? No, he didn't look like a diplomat. He didn't look like anything in particular. He was almost indescribable.

He now looked for the foreign-exchange counter, where five or six people were waiting, some Americans and two German women.

The Americans held out some traveler's checks, which they were asked to sign. After a glance to check their signatures, the cashier gave them some French banknotes. One of them started arguing about the rate of exchange and behind him two German women, mother and daughter, fidgeted impatiently.

It was almost twelve o'clock. Calmar was afraid the bank would close. He also remembered that he had left the parcel with the case in it on the seat of his car instead of drawing up in a side street, as he had intended to do, and putting it in the trunk. Well! The car was locked and a messily tied parcel would hardly attract thieves.

Two more people . . . one more . . . then he . . . He tried to stop his hand from trembling as he handed over the hundred-dollar bill. As he expected, the cashier looked at him in slight surprise, felt the note between his thumb and his forefinger to see whether it was thick enough, then held it up against the light.

"Just a minute, please . . ."

He stepped back to open a drawer on a level with his stomach, took out a slim list with columns of figures.

It all took only a few seconds, and there was now a group of young Italians awaiting their turn behind Calmar.

Once he had closed the drawer the cashier asked: "French currency, I suppose?"

"Correct."

The bills rustled in his fingers as he counted the

ten-franc notes by their corners because they were in wads, like the dollars and pounds in the briefcase.

Then he counted some smaller notes and finally some two-franc and one-franc pieces.

Calmar didn't bother to put the bills in his wallet, but stuffed them into his pocket. The dollars were not counterfeit! There was over one and a half million francs' worth of them in his briefcase placed negligently on the shelf of a cupboard in his apartment on Rue Legendre.

For the first time in his life he started spending money that did not belong to him. No—not true. He had stolen once, really stolen, deliberately. He must have been ten or eleven. It was hot, just as it was hot today. In that season he and his parents never went on vacation. On the contrary, it was the best time for business. After lunch his father used to drop off to sleep in the wicker chair in the kitchen and would wake up with a start when the shop bell rang.

He could no longer remember where his mother was that day. Maybe she was spreading the laundry on the garden lawn? Anyhow, he had slipped noiselessly behind the counter and had put his hand into the drawer where the money was kept. He had taken only fifty centimes. A few minutes later he bought an ice-cream cone from the Italian wheeling his little yellow cart through the streets.

He was walking along, licking the vanilla cream, when he saw one of his schoolmates in the distance. Since it wasn't Sunday and since he wasn't usually able to afford an ice-cream cone on weekdays, he had dropped the cone into the gutter and had then rushed down the street and turned the first corner he came to.

He went very red. He felt the blood throbbing in his temples. He had looked at himself in the mirror of a grocery and, since he was mystically inclined at the time, he had dashed off to church and gone to confession.

This time, in the back room of the Café de la Paix, he shouldn't have had a guilty conscience. He didn't want to have a guilty conscience. If he wasn't sitting outside for lunch, where it was cooler, it was because he didn't want to be seen by a member of the office staff or by a client, for he hardly ever frequented such expensive places.

Still, he ordered some very expensive dishes—hors d'oeuvres, half a lobster, broiled chicken livers, all dishes he rarely ate at home.

This was undoubtedly a further step, but it was inevitable. It wasn't out of greed but out of curiosity that he had changed the hundred-dollar bill at the bank.

Now he had in his pocket money he could not spend legally.

If he had bought an object that appealed to him, a cigarette case, for example, or a butane lighter, Dominique would have been surprised, just as she would have been surprised if he had given her a present or bought some toys for the children.

In any event, her calculations would never have been particularly precise. She didn't necessarily check on everything he spent, at least not out of distrust. She knew, of course, how much he earned, how much money he kept after giving her the money for the household expenses. Those five hundred francs had come from nowhere. He had to spend them before Saturday, since they didn't exist officially.

This began to bother him. He was fully aware of the sense of the word "began." He was aware of the inexorable chain of events, starting in Venice when he had watched a frozen image with his daughter at the center and had sensed the presence of a man near him who was looking at him appraisingly . . .

Not once since then had he really taken the initiative. His acts and gestures had proceeded one from the other without his taking any part in them.

Before going into the Café de la Paix he had inquired at the newspaper stand for the *Tribune de Lausanne,* which still hadn't arrived.

"In half an hour, perhaps . . ."

The thought struck him that he might be obliged to keep the one and a half million francs in his briefcase—the one and a half million francs that the old cleaning woman, who so hated the rich, all the rich, anyone who had a little more money or a little more spare time than she had, was far from suspecting existed.

Supposing . . . But of course, in the present state of affairs, with the knowledge he now possessed, there was no question of handing the money over to the police. He couldn't leave it in a bank, either, deposit it there and withdraw it when he at last found out to whom it belonged.

It would have been a fine gesture. He had thought of it for a moment as he ate his hors d'oeuvres. He would remain silent. He wouldn't tell anyone about the Venice train or about the case or about Arlette Staub. He would keep his secret stoically, despite the anxiety it was causing him, despite the suspicions that might weigh on him.

Then, one day, when the newspapers revealed the truth about the stranger on the train and the fortune left in an automatic locker at the Lausanne station, he would appear at the local police station, or better still, higher up the scale, at the criminal investigation department.

"I have brought the money . . . you can check it. It's all there except for a single hundred-dollar bill, which I thought I ought to change at a bank on Boulevard des Italiens to see whether or not it was counterfeit. . . ."

Why not? That might happen one day and everybody would congratulate him.

"You must understand that I couldn't have done otherwise. . . . Of course, I should have informed the police after leaving Arlette Staub's flat in Rue du Bugnon . . . but I was too stunned to do so, and I would probably have been less stunned if I weren't such an honest man. Ever since then I have had to . . ."

It was impossible to open a bank account without providing identity papers. And in some cases the banks even had to inform the income tax authorities about their clients' accounts.

To have a safe, too, he would have to show some documents, sign others.

A crazy idea . . . He had got to the lobster. He decided that he would throw the empty case into the Seine that evening, on his way home. Why not throw the money in at the same time? A shower of bank notes! Hundreds of thousands of francs, which would drift down the river . . .

It was impracticable. Nobody in his senses would get rid of a fortune like that.

He had overestimated his appetite and hardly touched the chicken livers.

"Waiter, could you ask at the newspaper stand whether the *Tribune de Lausanne* has arrived? . . . Yes, please get me a copy."

A blunder. The slightest detail might draw attention to him. It is just such unimportant facts that stick in people's memory and suddenly come back to them at the opportune moment.

"Oh yes! That very day a client eating a sumptuous meal asked me to buy him a copy of the *Tribune de Lausanne*."

Should he hide in order to read it? He looked through it as he drank his coffee, for he didn't order dessert.

No news items on the front page, no headlines,

nothing but reports on foreign affairs. On the second page, advertisements. On the third, a long article on the pollution of the Lake of Geneva and a report on the cantonal council.

The following pages carried news from the Valais, from the canton of Neuchâtel, from Geneva, and finally, from the canton of Vaud; a fire at Morges, a car crash at Cossonay, a cyclist run over at . . .

Lausanne: "Our Guests." Visit from a delegation of American teachers . . . car crash . . . unsuccessful burglary at a jeweler's shop in Rue de Bourg . . . a rude gentleman.

Then pages of sports news and, on the back page, more foreign affairs. Nothing about Arlette Staub. Nothing about the man who had disappeared in the Simplon tunnel (unless he got off the train at Brig!).

At any rate, he would now know on which page to look.

"The check, please, waiter . . ."

The newspaper hadn't solved any of his problems and he left it on the seat. It was half past one. Back at the Lido, Dominique and the children were leaving the boardinghouse to take their places on the beach. For everyone had to reserve his living space, as if by tacit agreement. You returned to find the same groups in the same spots. They ended up by smiling vaguely to one another.

"For heaven's sake, Josée, don't put your feet in the water before it's time to swim. . . ."

"How about me?" asked Bib, innocently.

"You, too, of course. If I tell your sister . . ."

"It's because I'm the contrary one, I know. You think I have all the faults. Other people don't wait two hours before putting their legs in the water or before bathing. . . ."

At lunch at the boardinghouse Dominique may have said:

"Right now, your father is lunching at Étienne's. I hope he hasn't ordered anything indigestible."

He went back to his car and remembered to put the attaché case with its broken locks into the trunk this time. He drove down the Champs-Élysées on his way to Avenue de Neuilly. Just before he got to the Ministry of Defense, he drew up in front of a light-yellow building with the inscription ASFAX—ROBUR—ROB, followed, in smaller letters, by "Incorporated."

The building had only two stories and some dormers, but it covered quite a large area. Before and during the war it had been a hardware shop in the old style, selling a wide variety of things: aluminum saucepans, casks of nails, bolts of every size, tools for every handicraft, wire netting for chicken runs, dumbbells, and curtain rods.

In those days old Baudelin was still alive, with a halo of white hair, invariably dressed in a long overall of the same gray as the iron he sold in one form or another.

His son, the present Joseph Baudelin, dressed in the same way as his father, and also lived in an aquarium-like atmosphere, for the enormous shop, which included a gallery, was illuminated by a glass partition giving onto the courtyard.

It was at the rear of this courtyard, in a sort of shed, that young Baudelin had carried out his first experiments. He knew nothing about plastics—except that they were being used increasingly in the manufacture of household utensils and all kinds of other articles.

Instead of consulting a specialist, he went to a friend, a chemist named Étienne Racinet, who made his living analyzing blood and urine. Racinet, a small and ruddy man, was a bachelor, always in high spirits, who often used to work in his laboratory late into the night.

Within a few weeks he had assembled and digested an enormous amount of information about the plastic products on the market at the time, and continued to add many new ones to his list, for a new material seemed to spring into existence every week: polyethylene, polypropylene, polystyrene, polycarbonate, et cetera.

"No problem about getting the basic plastic material; it's available as powder, granules, pellets, or liquid. But if you want to go into manufacturing plastic parts, you need an extruder or blender, because there are a number of ingredients to be added. And finally vessels to heat the mixtures to the proper temperature; and, of course, molding presses, blow-molding equipment, and the like."

"Do you need a lot of space for all that?"

"It depends on the size of the plastic parts you want to make."

Baudelin had started with molding small parts: toothbrush handles, spoons and forks for camping, beach pails, trowels, and rakes for children, eggcups, and napkin rings.

Only the shell of the old hardware shop remained. A modern ground floor with a fluorescent-light-paneled ceiling had become the showroom of the Asfax, Robur, and Rob products.

The offices were on the first floor, that is, the Paris offices; there were also offices at Nanterre and—the main one—at the factory in Brézolles.

Calmar ran up the marble staircase and stopped for a second in front of the glass door lettered "Reception."

"Has the boss arrived?"

"He came this morning and asked for you."

"But he knows I wasn't supposed to be back at work until this afternoon . . ."

"Have you forgotten what he's like, Monsieur Calmar?"

He wasn't a bad man, on the contrary. But he hated not to find people where he expected to find them. Each man at his desk. His dream, his ideal would be a world without Sundays, without vacations. Did he ever take a holiday?

A world without women and without children, too. How often did he go home, to the duplex on Boulevard Richard-Wallace, opposite the Bois de Boulogne, where his wife and daughter lived with four or five servants? Just about once a week, and he had barely set foot in the villa he had bought for his family on the Riviera.

He slept upstairs in an old storeroom, next to which he had built a rudimentary bathroom.

"Has he left for Brézolles?"

"You never know with him."

For Brézolles or for Nanterre. Or even for the new building sites in Finistère. You thought he was in the suburbs, and he would telephone from London or Frankfurt. That was his life. It was a part of Calmar's life, too, since he spent a good third of his time in the Avenue de Neuilly building.

"Home from the sea?"

That was the cheerful voice of Jouve, whom everybody called Bob, the clown, the comedian of the firm:

"Hey! You've put on some more weight! And where's your tan? Are you sure you went to Venice?" He frowned. "What's wrong, old man?"

Jouve was Calmar's only friend. Yet he felt obliged to reply with a forced smile:

"Nothing . . . the trip . . . that all-day train journey, with such crowded corridors that one couldn't even pee, then another all-night train ride."

"And your wife, the kids?"

"They stayed on. They're coming home on Saturday."

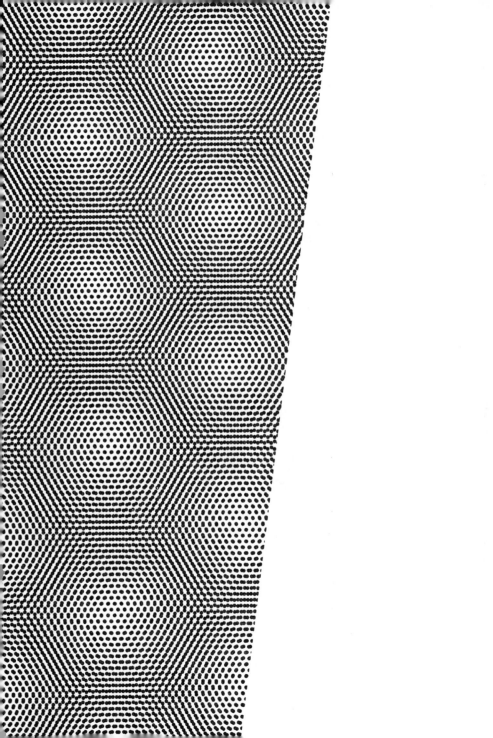

So far he had seen his concierge only twice, briefly each time. The same went for the garage owner. The others didn't count: the cashier in the bank on Boulevard des Italiens, who had only shown an interest in the hundred-dollar bill, satisfying himself that it was genuine; the headwaiter and the waiter at the Café de la Paix.

It was different now, and Bob's jokes worried him as he went into his office and found a stack of catalogues that had arrived from the United States in his absence.

Jouve was considered a lightweight who took nothing seriously and perpetuated the spirit of his student days at art school. The guy who couldn't see a typist without touching her fanny or her breasts, not even if it was Mademoiselle Valérie, the least attractive and most awkward of the lot, who felt obliged to scream with terror, as though he were trying to rape her.

He lived in a studio on Quai des Grands-Augustins. He had a succession of mistresses, a new one on an average of once a month. It was odd, because they all looked so alike—small, dark, with large, soft eyes. One wondered why he didn't keep the same one.

When he was joking, as he usually was, he looked like a large, fair-haired schoolboy with laughing eyes. Actually, he was the same age as Calmar. They had met when Calmar was still attending the Sorbonne and they both went to the same cheap restaurant on Quai des Tournelles, La Petite Cloche, where there was only one special dish daily, chalked up on a slate.

The proprietor had read in the papers that some of his colleagues had got rich by accepting canvases from young painters as payment for their meals, so he occasionally did the same thing with the art students.

Was Jouve still painting? He claimed he was and quite possibly it was true. But it was hard to distinguish between what he meant seriously and what he meant as a joke.

"Listen, my friend, I'm getting married. I am counting on you as my best man."

"To whom?"

"Aline, of course! We've lived together for almost three months now, and she's just told me that she's pregnant. So, since her father's a policeman in some village in Isère . . ."

He interrupted himself comically:

"One should always ask one's girl friend what her father is doing. A policeman! Not bad, is it? Why not a metropolitan policeman. . . ?"

That was months ago, sometime in the autumn. Around the beginning of January Calmar had asked him:

"How's Aline?"

"Aline? Which Aline?"

"The policeman's daughter . . ."

"Well, old man, to start with he wasn't a policeman but a road mender . . . and then one fine day she went off with some pimp she met at a dance. . . ."

"And the child?"

"I suppose there wasn't any child. In any case that's past history. You haven't met Françoise yet, have you? She's only been living with me for three weeks, but I think this is it. . . ."

Sometimes he had envied Jouve. But on closer observation he had reached the conclusion that his friend was less happy than he himself, and that if he joked about everything, he did so in order to hide his sadness.

Jouve was observing him, too. Particularly today. They had adjoining offices. Bob's was a sort of studio, with a large drawing table near the window, sketches pinned to the walls, incongruous objects, all made of plastic, cluttering the floor. The boss brought him new ones every week.

"Have a look at this bucket, Jouve. A competitor has just put it on the market. It's not bad but we can do better, by rounding off the edges for a start."

Rounding off the edges! That was his mania. Curiously enough it may also have been part of the secret of his success. Make plastic objects, whatever they were, look rounder, softer, more comfortable.

"When a pail or a basin or a toothbrush looks too sharp-edged, people think it must be junk."

Jouve came into Calmar's room in his shirt sleeves.

"It looks as though you're going to find lots of new things in the Sears Roebuck catalogue. . . ."

They both had strange jobs. Of course, like everyone else in the office, each had a special title. Jouve was art director, while Calmar had been appointed manager of the foreign-trade department.

It was an odd firm. Still, the system worked. Hadn't the head of the technical department, or, rather, of the laboratory, spent most of his life analyzing urine?

The customers were taken around the showroom on the ground floor, but were carefully kept away from the much-touted laboratories and research departments. The research departments consisted of Jouve's studio, though there were other ones, which looked more serious, with technicians who had been trained in technical colleges, in the factory at Nanterre, and, most important, in the modern factory at Brézolles, where two hundred men and women were employed.

Here, in Neuilly, was the brain center, with the boss's room, as bare as a cell, on the second floor, and a hole in the wall where Marcel, the chauffeur, would sleep when he didn't have time to go home at night.

The laboratory was still in the same old shed at the rear of the courtyard where everything had started and which had gradually been transformed. Plump little Monsieur Racinet went in for experiments that looked like children's games, testing the mixtures, the colors, operating the press with the sole assistance of the former storekeeper of the hardware shop, Cadoux, a Jack-of-all-trades.

"Hello, Justin . . ."

Bob was facing Calmar, an unlighted cigarette stub in his mouth.

"Are you sure you're feeling all right? Anything wrong between you and Dominique?"

"What could have gone wrong? I assure you . . ."

"All right! Don't get mad. You look upset, that's all. Is Dominique all right?"

"She's fine."

"Has she got a tan?"

"You know perfectly well that she doesn't tan. She gets red and peels."

There was a secret between them, a slightly embarrassing secret as far as Justin Calmar was concerned. When he was asked where he had met his wife he would answer lightly:

"In the subway, of all places . . . that's the one good thing about the subway. We took the same ride every day and we ended up by talking to each other."

It was a lie. He had met Dominique at La Petite Cloche when she was Bob's temporary mistress and worked as a salesgirl in a glove shop on Boulevard Saint-Michel.

Bob and she had separated. How Justin took over from his friend was a confused episode that he had never quite sorted out.

The main thing was that she had been his wife for thirteen years and that he was happy with her.

"I swear to God that I'm perfectly fine."

"Maybe! Maybe! But you don't look it."

"Do you think the boss will be coming in today?"

"Who cares?"

"Is Challans still on vacation?"

"Until the first of September."

Challans was manager of the trade department. Like the others, he had been given a professional title, but he must have been chosen because he dressed elegantly and soberly, looked impressive, and could talk endlessly on any topic, giving the impression of a very knowledgeable man.

In actual fact he had been a drug salesman who had been put in the best office in the building, complete with an anteroom staffed by a switchboard operator and two secretaries.

Challans entertained the clients and showed them around, leading them solemnly from object to object in the showroom. Usually, when he was discussing some business deal in his office, Baudelin, the boss, would come in looking inconspicuous and most people would take him for a member of the staff.

"Couldn't you allow the gentleman the credit facilities he is requesting, sir?"

It sounded like a joke. But nobody was less given to joking than Joseph Baudelin. Looking as he did, like an old family retainer, he noticed everything, was everywhere, and made every decision, here in Neuilly as well as in the factories.

He would often wander around department stores and other establishments with several branches, and would finger the objects on view like any other customer.

"Are you sure that this bucket can stand a temperature of eighty degrees, miss?"

"We have never had any complaints, sir."

"Doesn't the color fade after a few weeks on the shelves?"

"You can see for yourself . . ."

"How many do you sell a week?"

"I don't know. I'm not the sales manager."

He would buy it without saying who he was and would turn up in Bob's studio with a package under his arm.

"Have a look at this little horror. It's ugly but it sells. So if you can round it off and if Racinet can give it a better color that doesn't fade in the sunlight . . ."

Calmar suddenly realized that he had been happy in this firm and he told himself that there was no reason why he should stop being so.

"Where can I hide the bank notes?"

There was a huge cabinet with sliding doors in his office, where he put his catalogues. It had a lock, but since the cabinet had never been locked the key had been lost long ago.

In the left-hand corner near the window there was a green metal filing cabinet for his correspondence. The key was in the lock and every evening he simply slipped it into his drawer, which did not lock.

What *did* lock in the building? Nothing, probably, except for the small rosewood cabinet in which François Challans kept whisky, brandy, and port for his more important clients.

As for the laboratory in the courtyard, Racinet didn't consider his formulas original enough to be worth locking up.

Where could he hide a fortune of more than one and a half million francs? And how, if it were discovered, could he say it was his?

That was what he was thinking about as he pretended to study the illustrations in the American catalogues. This morning the notes in the briefcase had still been anonymous notes, which, for the time being, didn't belong to anybody.

For the time being. The proof was that he had thought for a moment, around midday, about the possibility of depositing them in a bank until further notice or of hiring a safe in which to store them.

Without realizing it, he started to think of that fortune as his own. He hadn't got as far as to wonder what he would do with it. He didn't have any plans. He was still quite vague about it all. It wasn't entirely his, but it was possible, if events were to take a particular turn, that it might become his.

Not by theft. Or by any dishonest act. He would be obliged to keep the money, that was all, just as he was obliged to hide it somewhere today.

The prospect was both seductive and agonizing. More agonizing than agreeable at the moment. Because nothing was definite yet. Because there were still some problems to be solved.

To start with, there was the problem of finding out what had happened to the man on the train from Venice and who he was. A spy, an international smuggler, as Calmar had good reason to suspect?

In that case to whom should he return the money? Could he go to the consulate of some country and say:

"I want to give you a sum of money that one of your agents deposited in a locker in the Lausanne station, to which he gave me the key"?

Why had he given him the key? To take the case to a certain Arlette Staub.

"When I arrived in her flat she was dead ..."

It was grotesque. And what if it were an international racket? Then to whom did the money belong? Not to the man from Venice, since the money had come into his hands illegally. The product of a theft, a swindle, or a fraud can never be considered the property of the author of the crime or of his accomplices.

Besides, who were his accomplices? Which accomplices?

At first sight his position had appeared to be almost

simple, but it became more complicated the more he thought about it, even if he did all he could not to think about it. He would have liked the boss to come into his office, to give him something urgent to do, something that would take up his time, day and night, for the entire week.

The accomplices . . . but there weren't only accomplices. Or, if there were, one of them had betrayed the others and had tried to act on his own by killing Arlette.

It was a very serious matter and he suddenly felt quite cold; he wanted to go and vomit that good, rich, heavy lunch to which he had treated himself at the Café de la Paix.

It was vitally important to sort things out.

The key first, an essential element, because whoever had it came into possession of one and a half million francs.

On Sunday, August 19, between Venice and Milan, that key had been in the pocket of the stranger who had given it to him on the pretext of catching a plane in Geneva and not having time to get off the train.

So, the temporary proprietor of the key between Milan and Lausanne was he himself, Justin Calmar.

Who knew about that? The man who had given him the key, of course. But there was no proof that nobody else knew. The train had been full for hours and there was every sort of person standing in the corridor. Anyone could have seen what was going on.

Why would the man have disappeared of his own free will? Why, for example, should he have committed suicide by jumping out of the train under the Simplon? And why, if he had done so, hadn't the morning's edition of the *Tribune de Lausanne* mentioned it? Calmar would look again the next day.

So he had disappeared! Somebody in Lausanne or elsewhere also knew about the existence of the attaché case, since the Staub girl had been murdered just before Calmar's visit.

Did whoever killed her know that she was going to receive the money, on trust probably, or hand it over to a third person?

So why had the crime been committed too soon? Half an hour, an hour, two hours later and the fortune would have been in the apartment on Rue du Bugnon.

Hell! He couldn't stand it any more. He was as worn out as if he had run around the Bois de Boulogne twenty times in the heat.

"You're green, old boy . . . if it's your digestion, you should take some bicarbonate of soda . . ."

Despite his frivolous appearance, Bob was too sharp to believe in indigestion. He must already have understood that his friend was obsessed by a problem, an insoluble problem!

Why, yes, why did the person who had got rid of Arlette Staub not get rid of Justin in his turn? Even if he didn't have the money any more!

If worst came to worst he would even have been prepared to put the bank notes back into the ruined attaché case and throw the whole thing into the Seine, some distance out of Paris, somewhere deserted.

How would that help him? If somebody—and this was perfectly plausible—knew that he possessed the cash, this somebody wouldn't know, couldn't imagine, that Calmar had suddenly decided to fling them into the river.

So? Where and when was he going to be in danger? At home? Somebody might already be hiding there. Not yet, because of Madame Léonard. But after five the apartment would be empty and anybody with the slightest skill would have no trouble in forcing the lock.

Even this was unnecessary. He would dine at Étienne's on Boulevard des Batignolles to please Dominique.

He would go home, switch on the light. A man would come upstairs and ring the bell. Would he refuse to answer the door, trying to make him believe that he wasn't at home when the light could be seen from the street?

Even here in the office he was not altogether safe. In a minute or two he would go down to the laboratory to see whether there was a hiding place for the money. On his return from vacation he also had to greet Racinet and Cadoux, whom he hadn't seen for two weeks.

In the time it would take him to cross the yard anyone could jump out at him or shoot him before he knew where the shot had come from.

That morning he had made a momentous discovery that affected him more than he had realized at the time: at home, in his own apartment, he, a man of thirty-five, married and with children, a man with responsibilities, did not have a single place where he could hide an object.

Wasn't it as though he had no right to any private, personal life?

In fact, it meant that he was a prisoner of his household. Not only could he not come in any time he pleased without saying where he had been, not only could he not spend money without his wife's knowing it, have a stomach-ache or be worried without it being remarked upon; he was also not even able to keep the smallest slip of paper to himself!

"Tell me, Daddy, what's in this box?"

Or:

"What's in this parcel?"

This applied even to the office, where he had always thought he had a certain freedom of movement. At least he could lock himself into the washroom. He did so, and at the mere sight of the toilet bowl he vomited his lunch.

"You look better already, man! Will you dine with me tonight at La Petite Cloche? I'll introduce you to

Françoise. She's a scream, you'll see. I've never met a girl with such a fund of dirty words. . . ."

"I'm afraid I'm not free tonight."

Bob frowned. He knew Dominique was away. He also knew that Justin had no other friend than himself and that the one time he was alone in Paris he would hardly be dining with his sister-in-law or at his parents-in-law's inn at Poissy.

Calmar, who had noticed Jouve's astonishment, added hurriedly:

"A guy I met in Venice and whom I promised . . ."

Oh dear! A blunder. The sort of blunder he must now be careful to avoid. Bob was capable of asking him quite innocently in front of Dominique:

"How about your friend from Venice. . . ?"

He corrected himself, making matters worse:

"When I say Venice . . . I really met him on the train. . . ."

"A Frenchman?"

"No . . . a Middle European, I'm not quite sure where from . . ."

He had reached the point of watching his every word, his every change of expression.

It was in a ridiculously out-of-the-way place, near Sartrouville, that he got rid of the attaché case, which few people would have been able to identify anyhow.

As the peak of irony he had first had to eat chicken livers, whether he liked it or not.

"So, Monsieur Calmar, how about your vacation? And that charming Madame Calmar?"

It wasn't quite dark when he went to Étienne's and the proprietor had come to shake his hand. He, too, had observed:

"You don't look very tanned for someone just back from vacation. You look rather ill . . . we'll give you something light: a consommé to start with, then a chicken-liver omelette that will make you smack your lips. . . ."

He even had to accept the omelet because the proprietor might well say, one day when he went there with Dominique:

"Do you remember your first dinner on your return from Venice when you didn't want my chicken livers?"

She would know that he hadn't lunched on Boulevard des Batignolles. From question to question, from lie to lie . . . he must be cautious!

Unless . . . A new idea crossed his mind, but he was reluctant to think about it seriously. Unless he told Dominique.

How would she react? She was certainly as honest as he was. She would start by reproaching him for not going to the police immediately.

He might persuade her that that was almost impossible once he had accepted the key from the stranger on the train. And now, tomorrow, the next day, it would be more impossible than ever, unless something unexpected happened.

He was increasingly convinced that the money should remain in his possession, come what may. And that if he mentioned it to his wife and she reached the same conclusions as he had (as she probably would), she would take over the management of their life.

"We must think of the children first, Justin. I always told you that the Paris air didn't do them any good. Remember, ever since the day we got married I said we should buy a little house in the country. There are some that you can pay for over a period of fifteen years. . . ."

All this because her parents had retired to Poissy!

"What were you doing when I met you? You were teaching English at the Lycée Carnot, weren't you? It was of your own free will, in order to earn more money, that you stopped teaching. You even thought of studying for an advanced teaching certificate.

"Well, now nothing is stopping you. We can settle anywhere, in a pleasant spot not far from a river. You could get a job in the nearby town.

"With no money problems you can do whatever you like. In the meantime, the children will lead a healthy life . . . we'll put some money aside for their education later on, because one never knows what may happen.
. . ."

No! That money which had made him suffer, and which would undoubtedly make him suffer still more, would never be used to satisfy the dreams of Dominique.

For one thing they weren't *his* dreams. Even, and above all, when they most looked as if they were. Advanced teaching certificate indeed! Admittedly it had crossed his mind. Admittedly there had been a period when he had seen himself as a professor in bedroom slippers, serenely preparing books on comparative linguistics or on some English poet—Byron, for instance, and his influence on world literature.

The truth of the matter was that he had chosen the teaching profession because a teacher in eighth grade had said:

"That boy is a born linguist."

Then he had obtained a scholarship. After getting a degree in literature, he had acquired degrees in English and German, which enabled him to teach on the high-school level.

That had been the time when he lived in the Latin Quarter, in a small hotel behind the Halle aux Vins and, on lucky days, had had his meals at La Petite Cloche, where he had met Robert Jouve.

His mother had been pleased to see him become a high-school teacher, regretting only that he was posted in Paris and not in Gien. She didn't realize that he was only an assistant to start with. As far as she was concerned it made no difference. She undoubtedly told her customers:

"My son, the professor . . ."

He hadn't let himself be pushed. As a matter of fact, nobody had tried to push him, but at the same time it couldn't be said that he had made a deliberate choice. He had drifted along with the tide, marrying Dominique and living with her in the two-room apartment overlooking the back yard on Boulevard des Batignolles, less than a hundred yards from the restaurant where he had just dined.

He had met the Lavaud family, who were then still living in the Calmars' present apartment, the father a headwaiter with an exalted idea of his social importance. The Wepler was still the meeting place of a certain number of movie stars, actors, and critics, who used to call him by his Christian name, Louis. He, for his part, referred to them by their Christian names also, as though they were equals.

"You see, my boy, in my job everybody knows you and you know everybody. There is no other profession in which one meets such interesting people. Not to mention the fact that one finds out much more about them than they think. If a man like me, with forty years' experience of Paris, would write his memoirs . . . You might teach my customers' kids, but you only know them superficially. . . ."

An older sister was married and lived in Le Havre. The other sister, Rolande, was the secretary of a lawyer on the Left Bank and lived by herself in somewhat mysterious circumstances.

Who knows? Although she appeared to be independent of her parents, Dominique might even suggest:

"Why don't we buy a restaurant like Daddy's?"

Because she was born to it. On Sundays at Poissy, when he went upstairs to have his siesta, she loved to lend a hand in the kitchen or the dining room. He would find her wearing an apron.

"There was just too much work for them, Justin. I had to pitch in. Since we don't pay for our meals . . ."

It wasn't he who wanted to go to Poissy every Sunday. It was all very well for the children because of the old horse. But he would have liked to have gone somewhere else from time to time.

And, as for teaching . . . It was odd to discover, suddenly, because a stranger had almost pressed a key into his hand, that nearly all his life had been based on half-truths, if not on lies.

He had been happy at the Lycée Carnot to begin with. Just like his father-in-law, he considered that his was one of the finest professions in the world.

He loved to see the rows of attractive faces in front of him and he was eager to teach the ninth and tenth grades, to communicate his admiration for English poetry to the young.

He hadn't stopped teaching because of the money, as he had told Dominique. Only Bob knew the truth.

The truth was that he had failed abysmally in his career as a teacher—and that he had failed after only two years, when his heart was still in it.

Yet he had done his best. Knowing the reluctance of most of his students to learn foreign languages, he had tried to make his lessons attractive. For example, he used to make up amusing conversations between his best students and himself.

"You look very serious today, Mr. Brown."

"It's because I forgot my umbrella."

"Is it raining?"

"How could it not be raining?"

They laughed. There was only one among them, always the same one, in the back row, Mimoune, who didn't laugh and who took no interest in what was going on.

"May I inquire what you are thinking about, Monsieur Mimoune?"

"Nothing, sir."

"I would like to remind you, Monsieur Mimoune, that at this particular moment you are supposed to be thinking about learning English. I presume that is what your parents sent you here for. . . ."

The boy was mulish and surly. At such moments his eyes expressed a mean resentment.

"Monsieur Mimoune, please translate the first sentence on page 65."

"I've forgotten my book, sir."

"Ask your neighbor to lend you his."

"I never borrow anything from anybody."

"Monsieur Mimoune, you will copy out page 65 three times."

It was ridiculous: a long-drawn-out battle between a mature man invested with authority over the class and a fourteen-year-old boy whose strength resided in the fact that his father was principal private secretary in an important ministry.

"Monsieur Mimoune . . ."

"Yes, sir?"

That "yes, sir" was so sardonic that Calmar often gave up.

"Nothing. Sit down. We'll try not to disturb your daydreams, provided you don't disturb us. . . ."

Calmar had no difficulty with the other classes. But in Mimoune's class things gradually degenerated and two groups started to form.

He could tell from the laughs. The time came when his jokes worked with only half the class and then with an ever smaller proportion.

"Well, gentlemen, if you prefer severity I shall be severe . . . to my great regret, I should add."

He only taught the ninth and tenth grades. The year that Mimoune passed on to the eleventh grade, despite his bad marks in English, it so happened that Justin was appointed to teach that grade.

The boy was no longer a child. His voice had changed. In his eyes there was not only a tenacious kind of spite but also an irresistible urge to have the last word.

"Monsieur Mimoune . . ."

"Yes, sir."

"You have your textbooks?"

"Yes, sir."

"Be so kind . . ."

"It won't be because I'm kind, sir. It'll be because I have to . . ."

"Though it gives me no pleasure to do so, I congratulate you on your subtlety. I only wish you would apply it more lavishly when translating the text. Page 42, please . . ."

Calmar had twice been summoned by the headmaster. Mimoune's name was never mentioned. The headmaster spoke of parents in general, rather vaguely.

"There have been some complaints about a certain laxity in your classes, Monsieur Calmar. It appears that you rather like to make your students laugh, even at the expense of discipline, and that at other times you are excessively severe. Think about it. Don't forget the golden mean . . . it's up to you, Monsieur Calmar."

The slap came in June of his third year of teaching. Josée was a year and a half old and was teething. The weather was sultry. Calmar's parents-in-law hadn't yet left Paris, and his wife and he lived in the two rooms on Boulevard des Batignolles. Dominique had been in poor health all through the spring.

Mimoune proved both more self-confident and more virulent than ever before.

"Monsieur Mimoune, I have already told you that I have forbidden the use of chewing gum in class. . . ."

"I should point out, sir, that you have set a precedent by constantly sucking peppermints."

This was true. At the time Calmar often suffered from indigestion and hated to think that his breath was bad when he spoke to his students.

"I do not permit you to . . ."

"And I will not tolerate a . . ."

They were both talking at the same time, a yard away from each other, and Mimoune, who had stood up, was now as tall as his teacher. Who was the first to make a gesture that the other one misunderstood? A slap resounded, followed by a hush the like of which the students had never heard before, followed, in its turn, by a riot.

"I assure you I felt I was in danger, sir," Calmar told the headmaster.

"He looked at me with such fury that when he unfolded his arms I thought he would . . ."

"Please, Monsieur Calmar . . . let him speak. . . ."

"He hit me, sir. I know he has been wanting to hit me for a long time. He's hated me for three years."

"What do you say to that, Monsieur Calmar?"

"I agree that for three years this student . . ."

What was the point? He had lost. And Mimoune wasn't the only one to blame. The others had joined in. The other teachers, the supervisors, even the headmaster eyed him with suspicion, as though he were a black sheep.

He had started teaching with joy, with genuine enthusiasm.

"It's a bust, I was only reprimanded. But sooner or later it'll be worse. I'll be sent to some backwater in the provinces until the day when I'm advised to re-sign. . . ."

"What are you going to do?"

"I don't know. I can't see myself as an interpreter at Cook's or as a receptionist in a hotel. And yet that's all I'm equipped to do. . . ."

"But don't you know German, too?"

"About as well as English . . ."

"I'll have a word with my boss about it."

"Do you think there's any room for me in the plastics business?"

"You don't know Baudelin. Is he an industrialist? Absolutely not. He's an ironmonger and he doesn't know anything about plastics. What am I? A painter and a former art student, but that didn't stop him from employing me to design bowls, toothbrushes, spoons and forks, and unbreakable bottles.

"As recently as last week he complained that nobody in the firm could speak English. 'These bloody Americans,' he said, 'have better models than we have and they invent new plastic objects every day. If only somebody could read their catalogues . . .'"

That was his job now. Everything had started with the catalogues of Sears Roebuck, Macy's, Gimbel's, and other department stores.

Dominique was as convinced as her parents that he had stopped teaching in order to earn more money.

"I know you're making a sacrifice, Justin, you're doing it for Josée and me." (Bib wasn't born then.) "It isn't too bad, is it? Are you sure you won't regret it?"

"Of course not, darling . . ."

What was he going to have to do to make things plausible to her from now on? He thought about it in bed, their bed, where he felt uneasy by himself, obses-sed by the idea of the briefcase full of cash in the hall closet, casually placed there like an object of no value.

And if . . . ?

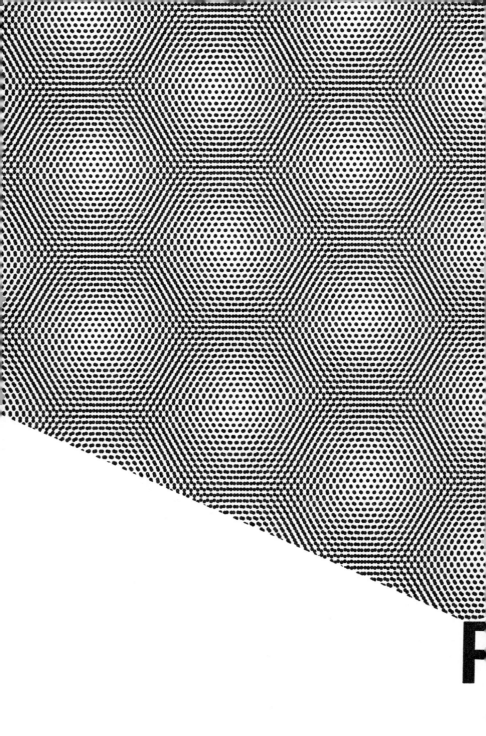

F

ART TWO

"My poor Justin! You don't look at all well. I hope you had your meals at Étienne's and that he took good care of you."

Ever since they had met at the station on Saturday, she had kept her eyes on him anxiously.

"Have you been taking your liver capsules regularly?"

That was an old story dating from his long battle with Mimoune at the Lycée. He had been particularly worried at the time because he could see no alternative to teaching and felt he wouldn't hold out for long. His digestion had borne the consequences. They already had Dr. Bosson as their family doctor, but it wasn't Bosson who had mentioned his liver; it was Dominique.

"Don't you think he has a weak liver, doctor?"

Since Bosson never contradicted anyone, he had nodded and muttered vaguely:

"Maybe slightly."

He had prescribed capsules for him, to be taken first thing in the morning and after meals. Justin would forget to take them for months on end.

"You should be careful. You're turning yellow again."

It was odd to see them again, to see his daughter in a dress, more tanned than when he had left her, and Bib, who suddenly looked like a big boy.

He didn't feel altogether at ease with them. As for them, they sensed vaguely—or, rather, Dominique did —that something had changed.

"Did you go out much in the evenings?"

"Only once, with Bob."

"Did you come home late?"

"At eleven. The other nights I was in bed by ten. . . ."

"Did Madame Léonard come in every day, as I asked her?"

"I suppose so. I didn't see her, but everything had been tidied up when I got back in the evening."

"You haven't had any trouble at the office?"

"Not the slightest."

He had to get used to it, to readjust.

A number of little things had happened throughout the week, but he could not mention them. On Tuesday he had bought the *Tribune de Lausanne* at a booth in the Champs-Élysées. He had stuck it into his pocket, gone into a *bistrot* and, after ordering a drink, had looked through the paper in the washroom.

He couldn't run the risk of being seen reading a Swiss paper, he who, in his whole life, had spent less than three hours in Switzerland and didn't have any friends or relatives there.

There was some news under the heading "Valais" and his heart started to beat faster.

"A Mutilated Body Under the Simplon

"On Sunday night some workmen checking the line made a sinister discovery in the Simplon tunnel. Three miles from Brig they found the appallingly mutilated remains of an unidentified middle-aged man scattered on the track. It is assumed that he was a passenger who opened the wrong door while in the tunnel and lost his balance.

"Numerous trains go through the Simplon in the vacation season, especially on Saturdays and Sundays, and at the present stage of the investigation it is impossible to know from which train the unfortunate passenger fell."

No headlines. No special emphasis, except for "appallingly" and "unfortunate passenger." It was just another news item. It might be mentioned again and it might not.

What mattered was that the stranger on the train

from Venice would not come to reclaim the contents of the attaché case from Justin. There was no reference either to his passport or to the contents of his wallet, which was rather strange, unless the man or men who had pushed him into the tunnel had removed them before committing the crime.

Two pages later another heading, in the same small print:

"Lausanne Manicurist Found Strangled

"Late Monday afternoon, the police were called to an apartment on Rue du Bugnon, where a tenant, Juliette P., a dressmaker, had been puzzled by the silence in the apartment next door.

"Finding the door unlocked, she had opened it and discovered her neighbor lying dead in the living room. The person in question is a certain Mademoiselle Arlette Staub, born in Zurich, who had been living for some years in Lausanne.

"Arlette Staub had been employed, over an unusually long period of time, as a manicurist in the beauty salon of one of Lausanne's best-known hotels, frequented by an international clientele.

"Yet it seems that the young woman, who was pretty and elegant, was not content with her salary and received a considerable number of visitors in her apartment.

"Although the police have been uninformative about the matter, it would appear that the twenty-five-year-old manicurist was strangled on Sunday afternoon with a blue silk scarf, which was found next to her body."

That was all. Not too much emphasis here, either. Nor any compassion for the "elegant" young woman who was "not content with her salary" and who "received a considerable number of visitors in her apartment."

Yet there was one detail that worried him: "The police have been uninformative about the matter. . . ."

Didn't that mean that the police were in possession

of at least one clue that they didn't want to disclose? Had someone noticed a man in a cream-colored suit late on Sunday afternoon, who had stopped in front of the building and had got back into his taxi a few minutes later?

Had the taxi driver been traced? Had he given the police a description of Calmar and mentioned his brief-case?

At the station buffet the waitress must surely remember him, his two whiskies, his worried and distraught look. . . .

From now on all that was a part of his life. He had almost adapted himself to it. On Monday evening he had gone as far as Sartrouville to throw the case, wrapped in blue paper, into the Seine. It had floated for a while before sinking into the water.

He had been suspicious of everything, of the cars parked in the dark that might be concealing courting couples, of the barges moored along the embankment, of the tramps sleeping at the foot of a tree, even of the pier of a bridge.

He had made sure that he ate all his meals at Étienne's, except the evening when he had gone to dinner with Bob and his new mistress, Françoise of the dirty words, who must have exclaimed after he left:

"Your friend isn't much fun, is he!"

He had never been much fun. But, apart from the darkest period at the Lycée Carnot, he didn't think he had been gloomier than anyone else. In the evenings he helped Josée with her homework and she had no compunction about teasing him, something she wouldn't have dared had he been peevish or pompous.

No. He was like other people, like most other people. Wasn't he now behaving as any other person would have behaved in his circumstances?

Lack of a secure hiding place in the office or in the laboratory on Avenue de Neuilly had forced him to a solution that only half satisfied him and that he considered temporary.

Since he had found the case in an automatic locker in a railroad station, why shouldn't he continue to use the same system?

On Tuesday he had left the office earlier than usual and had crossed nearly the whole of Paris to go to a shop selling leather goods on Boulevard Beaumarchais. He couldn't risk purchasing something that might appear incongruous in the neighborhood where he lived, but he had remembered seeing this particular shop one day as he was driving by, almost on a level with the Cirque d'Hiver.

Only the size mattered, not the quality. Indeed, the case needed to be quite nondescript so that people wouldn't notice it every time he went to pick it up.

Because, from now on, he would have to pick it up every five days. That was the rule. After five days the lockers were opened by the man in charge of the left-baggage office and the contents kept on the shelves of the left-baggage office for a period of six months.

He didn't want to risk that. He could have hired a locker for a longer period, but he would have had to fill in a form with his name and address.

He started with Gare Saint-Lazare. He had to retrieve the case by Sunday or put some more money in the slot, which he thought was dangerous. He preferred to change stations each time.

All this was far more complicated than it had seemed at first. Never until his return from Venice had he realized that he was the prisoner of a routine and that for twenty-four hours a day his acts and gestures were observed either by his wife and children or by his boss, colleagues, and the typists at the office.

The proof of it was that he had never heard so many people commenting on how ill he looked. He had no right to have indigestion, to be worried or bothered.

"What's wrong, old man?"

Dominique would get up from the table to get his little capsules.

"If you're not feeling better in two or three days, I'm going to call Dr. Bosson. . . ."

The doctor lived three houses away, and one could see him walk by holding his old bag, such a heavy bag that he always looked as if one of his shoulders were higher than the other. He had a large grizzly mustache, which made him look like a spaniel; when he was examining a patient, he muttered between his teeth.

He liked the Calmars, especially Josée, whom he had ushered into the world. Maybe he liked all his patients?

Justin had no desire to be examined by the doctor; before his wife got even more worried, he managed to recover some of his poise. Things were improving. He could already visualize fairly calmly what he could do and what he couldn't do, what he could say and what he couldn't say.

Monsieur Baudelin, too, had been involved. On Tuesday he had burst into Calmar's office.

"What, back already?"

As though he didn't know that he himself had insisted on Justin's return to work on Monday afternoon!

"You certainly don't look as if the vacation has done you much good. Anyway, vacations are no help to anyone. You kill yourself trying to overtake trucks, you sleep in nasty rooms, you stuff yourself with all sorts of things, thinking that just because you aren't eating at home the food must be better. Then you spend your time getting sunstroke, quarreling with your wife or shouting at your children, and, when you finally get back, you take a rest at the office. Rest, my friend! You have plenty of time. As for me, I haven't been on vacation and I hope I won't have to. . . ."

Had it not been for Saturday afternoons and Sundays Baudelin would undoubtedly have been a happy man. But on those days he was out of sorts.

One Saturday afternoon when Calmar had come back to the office to get a file he was proposing to work on on Sunday, he had found the offices empty and silent. They had depressed him. The building looked as though it had been abandoned and everything that had seemed important during the week suddenly appeared futile.

The showroom, for instance, with all its plastic objects of every color, turned into the caricature of a shop. The filing cabinets lost their solemnity, and the typewriters, hidden under their covers, had something funereal about them.

It was hard to believe that on other days the whole building was humming, that people came and went with a preoccupied look, concentrating on those yellow or green buckets, those transparent covers, those bottles and combs, all those objects that were the fruit of endless research, discussion, experimentation in the laboratory and that suddenly looked absurd.

Justin had been seated at his desk looking for the papers he needed when he heard a typewriter clicking upstairs. This intrigued him, so he went up to the second floor, where he rarely set foot.

He found the boss, in pajamas and dressing gown, typing with two fingers on a portable typewriter that Calmar had never seen before.

"What are *you* doing here on a Saturday afternoon?"

"I'm sorry. I came to look for some documents that I wanted to translate in my spare time at home."

"Are you working overtime at the moment?"

He looked sullen but Calmar felt that Baudelin, who was an old man already, was not displeased to see a human being. He must have spent the weekend wandering about the empty offices, the laboratory, the warehouses. This became obvious on Monday, when he called one of the typists and dictated the result of his observations in the form of brief memoranda for the various departmental managers.

While the offices on the first floor were modern and comfortable, Baudelin's office was a sort of storeroom; no client had ever entered it. There were green filing cabinets and the walls were lined with white wooden shelves stuffed with every sort of catalogue and paper. On the floor, in the corners, were piled the products of the firm, above all the unsuccessful products that had been used in Bob's or Monsieur Racinet's research work.

On Sunday morning the boss frequently would get his chauffeur, Marcel, to drive him to Nanterre or to the factory at Brézolles, where he would find only the watchman and would roam through the empty offices as he did here.

Since they had started building in Finistère, he sometimes spent the night in the car; on Sunday, people driving by would see him coming and going, all alone, under the cranes and past the gaping holes, cement mixers, and crushing machines.

"I hope your wife got more out of her stay in Venice than you did."

"She's not coming back until Saturday."

He had seen her only once, on the firm's twentieth anniversary, when all the staff had been invited to a buffet supper in the showroom. He remembered faces and names. He never forgot anything. Thus he remembered that Justin had spent his vacation in Venice; he always knew the whereabouts of each of his employees.

He might have had more difficulty in telling what his own wife and daughter were doing.

I have to watch myself with him, Justin thought.

He didn't see the boss frequently, usually just for a

few minutes, in the doorway, but he was the most dangerous of them all.

Bob looked at him more closely and asked him questions as though he were worried about him. But Bob would soon reach the only conclusion he considered normal.

"All marriages are destined to go wrong," he liked to say, as though he were joking. "The minute you put two human beings together, a male and a female, it's absurd to think that one of them is going to sacrifice his or her personality forever."

Bob had never lived with a woman for more than three months. Did he regret it? Wasn't his pessimism a result of his incapacity to form part of a real couple?

"For a while you go along hand in hand or arm in arm. You talk to each other. We all like to talk about ourselves and only lend half an ear to what the other person is saying. The second or third time that the woman starts to tell the same story about her childhood, irritation sets in, and the same thing happens if the man recalls what he did when he was seventeen."

He concluded:

"It's like a boxing match. In the end one of the two must win and the other one knuckle under. The question is, who's it going to be?"

Justin had the impression that in his marriage neither party had tried to win. Only now did he become aware of the narrow limits in which his life was enclosed.

Simply in order to put the briefcase into another locker he had to think up an excuse, either at the office, if he left earlier than usual, or at home, if he returned later than usual.

The few occasions on which he had stopped on the way home in the past had been to buy the first violets of the season for Dominique—he always brought her the first violets and had done so for thirteen years. Or else he would bring something for the children, the first cherries, the first apricots, the first peaches, sometimes a cake in the winter, which he always bought in the same pastry shop on Avenue de la Grande-Armée.

"I'm sorry, my dear, I'm slightly late. I was held up by an accident right in front of my car and it's a miracle they didn't stop me as a witness . . . I pretended not to have seen anything. . . ."

He couldn't make up accidents every five days. It would work out in the end, of course. It was a question of perfecting the system, of organization, as François Challans, enamored of the word "efficiency," would say pompously.

The man on the Venice train was dead. Arlette Staub, the manicurist of easy virtue (according to the *Tribune de Lausanne*) was also dead. In neither case had there been any mention of the attaché case or the money. Nor any mention of espionage or of an international racket.

The one and a half million francs didn't belong to anyone until further notice, which was as much as to say that they belonged to Justin Calmar.

And, unless he were forced to do otherwise, Calmar had every intention of keeping them. Once again, it was not out of greed; he just didn't have the slightest idea of what to do with them. He had only changed one note and he had had difficulty in spending it.

"Well, you've bought yourself a new tie!"

"I thought you might like to see me wearing a somewhat gayer tie. . . ."

It was she who usually chose his ties, the inevitable present on his birthday, for Christmas, or on Father's Day. He hadn't been able to resist the temptation of buying himself a tie with red and blue stripes at a haberdashery on Avenue George V, where he would never have set foot before.

"It must have been expensive."

"Less expensive than I thought . . . eighteen francs."

It wasn't true. It had cost twenty-five. And he already regretted having lied. He must be more careful and more alert in the future. The name of the shop was on the inside of the tie. Suppose Dominique went into the same shop on his next birthday and asked for a tie costing eighteen francs?

He had worked all his life. As a child he had worked harder than his schoolmates in order to get a scholarship, and as a teacher he had taken more trouble than his colleagues, though that had not prevented him from failing pitiably because of a boy called Mimoune.

He had to get his own back secretly, since he couldn't admit to anyone that he had become a rich man.

As the days and the weeks went by, his wife became more attentive, more protective. She constantly watched him out of the corner of her eye.

"You're sure you don't have any problems you're keeping from me?"

"I assure you, darling . . ."

"Well, it must be exhaustion then."

"I assure you I'm not working any harder than usual."

On Sundays he noticed that his parents-in-law, too, had started glancing at him, and his family must have been discussing him behind his back. The proof was that one Sunday morning, while he was taking his daughter for a walk near their apartment (Bib was at home with a cold), she suddenly said to him, with the serious expression of an adult:

"We're all terribly selfish, really."

"Who do you mean?"

"Us, the women . . . children, too . . ."

"Why do you say that?"

"Because we're so used to men working that we take

it for granted. We're always asking for something. Last week I wanted Mother to buy me a new sweater for the autumn. I pretended that last year's was too tight, though in fact it still fits. The truth is that I wanted a light-blue sweater like my friend Charlotte. That means more work for you. . . . Will you forgive me for being so selfish?"

Even she was becoming protective and showed concern when he didn't take a second helping at dinner.

"Aren't you hungry?"

"I've had enough."

"Are you sure you're eating enough for a man like you?"

"Yes, darling, of course."

Mademoiselle Denave, too, the most unattractive of the secretaries, the one Bob slapped on the behind to make her blush every time he passed her in the corridor, seemed to have transferred to him the silent adoration that she used to lavish on his friend.

Whenever he went into the secretaries' room in search of an available typist, she was the first to stand up, even when she was in the middle of a letter.

"Do you need me, Monsieur Calmar?"

Her or anyone else. She treated him with more obsequiousness than any of the others, as though he were the most important figure in the firm.

"Is everything all right, Monsieur Calmar?"

"Yes, yes, of course."

This solicitude, this spying on him, was irritating. He felt himself imprisoned by a row of eyes observing everything he did, his every expression, as much in the office as at home.

One day, in a letter to an American chemical firm in which he was inquiring about a new synthetic base, he made a mistake in the next-to-last paragraph. It was five to six when he finished dictating the letter to Mademoiselle Denave, and no sooner had he got into his car than he realized that he had used an incorrect term that had changed the entire sense of the letter. He resolved to correct it the next day and repeated to himself as he dropped off to sleep that night:

"Don't forget to tell Denave . . ."

Well, the next day, when he found the letter on his desk and ran through it, he noticed that his mistake had been corrected.

"Mademoiselle Denave, would you come here a minute, please."

"Yes, Monsieur Calmar . . ."

He looked at her severely.

"This is the letter I dictated to you last night, isn't it? Tell me . . . is this precisely how I dictated it?"

"I . . ."

"You haven't changed a word?"

"I'm sorry, Monsieur Calmar . . . I thought you were tired. You used one word instead of another and I took the liberty of correcting it. . . ."

"And what if that was the word I intended?"

She lowered her head as if she were about to cry.

"Do you mind not doing that any more and not assuming that I'm tired? I'm feeling fine, Mademoiselle Denave . . . very fine indeed. Far better than some people think."

He was making a mistake. He mustn't repeat the Mimoune episode with this poor girl who was taking him under her wing. But why did she think he needed protection? Against what? Against whom?

On the contrary, he was in the process of organizing himself. Now that the immediate danger seemed over he left the bag in the same locker every other time and simply slipped some more money into the slot.

He had found two more newspaper stands where he could buy the *Tribune de Lausanne,* one of them on Place de l'Étoile, which meant that he didn't have to go a great distance. Nevertheless, he went into a café or bar and shut himself into the washroom to read the paper.

The man of the Simplon tunnel was no longer mentioned, as if the Swiss police no longer attached any importance to the incident. Unless, of course, the opposite were true. When the police are silent about a case, it sometimes means that it is so important they do not want to draw people's attention to it. Surely such silence would also be observed if there were political implications?

There was no further mention of Arlette Staub, either. The news consisted mainly of local parades and some car accidents; what happened in Switzerland on Sunday, August 19, might as well never have taken place.

Still, he was suspicious. He remembered a case the newspapers had described at length a few years earlier, the name of which reminded him of one of the details of his own case (to the extent to which one could call his a case): Briggs or Bricks . . .

The newspapers reported that there was an important firm in the United States that organized the transfer of funds for banks and large industries with armored trucks and teams of private policemen.

Some crooks had watched the movements of the armored trucks of the Boston agency for weeks and months, and discovered that for a few hours every day large sums of money were locked into the office before being transferred.

The agency's offices constituted a fortress, and the crooks took more than a year to plan the robbery. At the time, it had been called the boldest and most important robbery of the century.

He couldn't recall the details, but four or five men finally managed to get hold of five or six hundred thousand dollars and disappear without a trace.

For years the police worked in silence. They began

to suspect a few men who frequented one of the water-front bars; day after day, these men had been shadowed.

Not one of them spent a single dollar that he had not come by legitimately. Not one of them had gone in for any extravagant spending.

All the banks and all the department stores had the numbers of the notes. For almost ten years not a single stolen bank note had been put into circulation, in America or abroad.

According to Massachusetts law, in crimes where there was no bloodshed no legal action could be taken against the criminal if he was not caught within ten years. There were just a few more weeks and the time limit would expire.

It was then that a small local bank reported a ten-dollar bill whose number was on the list. Through the shopkeeper who had deposited it, one of the suspects was traced and, exactly five days before the expiration of the time limit, the whole gang was arrested.

And so the five men had held out, living in penury, for years on end, while their fortune had been buried in a cemetery, if Calmar remembered rightly. Only one of them had been unable to resist at the last moment. His child or his wife had been ill. He had gone to fetch a few bank notes in the middle of the night. . . .

Calmar never forgot the story. He certainly wasn't a crook. He hadn't stolen anything. It wasn't he who had pushed the man out of the train from Venice into the Simplon tunnel. It wasn't he, either, who had strangled the manicurist with a blue silk scarf just as she was dressing to go out.

Chance had simply placed in his hands a fortune that belonged to nobody. As he thought about it more and more, he reached a still more optimistic conclusion.

It was unquestionably true that the stranger on the train had chosen him deliberately. Otherwise, why would he have questioned him so insistently about himself—his family, his work, his tastes, his habits—during most of the journey, to the point where Justin was cross with himself for having spoken so much, for letting himself be pumped like that, for having answered so willingly while he himself had not asked a single question?

Wasn't it obvious by now that so detailed an interrogation did not correspond to what Calmar had at first believed to be a perfectly simple errand, an errand (he remembered thinking) that could have been performed by the first person handy? One of the porters, for instance, could have done it just as well.

And if his companion had been vague about the plane he was catching, was it not because the plane didn't exist?

Either he knew that he would commit suicide in the darkness of the Simplon tunnel, or he was running a risk of which he was well aware and he foresaw that he would never reach his destination.

Besides, is it natural suddenly to go to the washroom in a train that is rushing through one of the longest tunnels in Europe, unless one feels an urgent need? Not once between Venice and Milan nor between Milan and Domodossola had the man shown any such pressing need.

Did he have a mysterious appointment at the end of the corridor or in another compartment? Wasn't suicide the most likely hypothesis? Wouldn't that explain why he hadn't been identified? Hadn't he taken care, before he jumped, to destroy his papers and the passport that Calmar had seen him holding at the Italian frontier?

If he had chosen Justin instead of looking for another passenger—and the train was full of them—was it not because he knew that the mission wasn't as simple as it looked?

Did he foresee the possibility of Arlette Staub's death? And, in that case, did he not prefer to avoid a scandal, avoid having other people implicated? And other people might indeed be implicated if Calmar went to the police and blurted out the whole story.

He rather liked this version. He improved it gradually, and every day it became more likely. He added frills here and there, like the fact that at a certain point, just before giving him the key, the stranger had looked him straight in the eye and said:

"I know that you're an honest man. . . ."

Why wasn't this true? It became true.

It was true. There were a number of sentences that had gone unheard owing to the noise of the train and the wind beating against the curtain. He was almost sure that these words had been uttered.

Besides, that hardly mattered any more. He had overcome the problem of guilt. He had decided once and for all that he was not guilty and the problem no longer existed.

Nevertheless, there were a number of worries that could not be eliminated so easily. On Sunday, for instance, when they were driving to Poissy as usual. His wife was sitting next to him and observed that the trees were turning red. Then, a few hundred yards farther on, she sighed:

"It's incredible how the cost of living has risen again this year. . . ."

He didn't answer; the remark didn't call for an answer. But he felt that something else would follow.

"I was on Avenue de Wagram yesterday and passed a shop that isn't particularly expensive. I saw a fall suit, russet, very plain, very pretty, I must say, rather like the Chanel suits. Well, it was the same shop where I bought my green wool dress last year. I went in and asked what it cost . . . guess."

"I don't know."

"Three hundred and twenty-nine francs! Three hundred and twenty-nine francs for a little two-piece suit that you see on virtually everybody. . . ."

"Did you buy it?"

"Are you mad? Don't you realize?"

"You should have bought it if you liked it . . . you should go and get it tomorrow."

Just over three hundred francs! What was a sum like that to him now, a man who had over one and a half million francs?

"What are you talking about? Have you lost all sense of the value of money? You're forgetting that I'll have to buy a whole set of new clothes for the children this winter. They've grown tremendously. . . ."

He suddenly felt sorry for her, sorry for them all. He had lived for years without being aware of how badly off they were. Of course, in his childhood he had wanted lots of things that his parents couldn't afford, especially after his father's death. Even ice-cream cones were limited exclusively to Sundays, and he couldn't remember ever having eaten one on a weekday, except the one he stole for, unless it was a great feast day.

He had worn coarser, thicker shoes than most of his schoolmates because they lasted longer, and he had been allowed to have a new suit only once a year, and an overcoat every two years, even if the current one no longer fitted properly.

At the beginning of their marriage they had had a number of difficulties, especially at the end of the month, and the occasions on which they had treated themselves to lunch or dinner at Étienne's, a cheap enough restaurant, were few and far between.

He preferred not to think about it, not to know about it, but he was almost sure that sometimes, toward the twenty-fifth or twenty-sixth of the month, his wife had borrowed a small sum from her parents "to make ends meet."

And now, after thirteen years, poor Dominique still had to do without a suit that she must have gazed at for ages in the window before daring to go into the shop! She must have asked the price before trying it on, and murmured in embarrassment:

"I'll come again with my husband."

He even felt sorry for Josée, who admitted having asked for a sweater even though she didn't really need one and who consequently thought she had added to his worries and his exhaustion.

"What are you thinking about, Justin?"

"Nothing . . . I'm looking at the car ahead of us and wondering whether it's going to pass the truck. . . ."

"How's Bob?"

"Very well, as always."

"Has he got a new mistress?"

"I don't know. I haven't been out with him since you came back from Venice . . . you know that."

"You might have seen her outside the office."

"Do you think she waits for him on the other side of the street, like mothers who pick up their children at school?"

"No, but when you have a drink together . . ."

The alarm signal was flashing.

"What do you mean?"

He tried to play for time to think.

"Don't you sometimes have a drink with him on your way home?"

She must have smelled his breath. It was true that every time he read the *Tribune de Lausanne* he had a drink.

"I do have a drink from time to time, but not necessarily with Bob."

It had to be with someone she was not in the habit

of seeing. They occasionally spent the evening with Bob, not very often, admittedly, but once might be too much.

"I'm a bit angry with you, Jouve, for debauching my husband. . . ."

Since she had married Calmar, Dominique always addressed Jouve rather formally.

"With me, Dominique?"

He didn't go as far as to call her "Madame." After all, he had lived with her for two or three months.

"That drink you have together every day . . ."

Dangerous! Everything was dangerous, even his breath!

"You forget that there's a bar in Challans' office and that whenever he's in a good mood he likes to give us the same treatment as his clients. . . ."

"He must be in a very good mood these days . . . his vacation must have done him more good than yours did you. By the way, where does he go?"

"To Saint-Valery-en-Caux. He has a small yacht and spends most of his time at sea."

"With his wife?"

"He never told me."

"Will I have time to ride before lunch, Daddy?"

"Yes, darling."

He would soon be sleeping in one of the rooms above the dining room. There was always that to be thankful for.

Some weeks were painful, agonizing, in the office and at home. Sitting at the dinner table, he would suddenly feel his forehead bathed in sweat, his nerves knotted, a sense of constriction in his chest; at moments like these, he couldn't bear to have anyone look at him.

He gradually succeeded in persuading himself that the money was his, that he had earned it legitimately, that it was unjust, revolting, not to be able to touch it, not to buy the smallest object that he had coveted for years and wanted to give his wife or his children.

He sometimes even wondered whether the bank notes were still in the case.

Of course, though the key to the locker changed every five days (the locker being almost invariably in a different station), he kept it in his pocket; he was always afraid that Dominique might ask him what it was for.

An official opened all the lockers after a certain period of time in order to put the contents in the left-baggage office, which meant that there were either duplicate keys or a master one. One of the officials who had seen Justin several times in the same station might be curious enough to open his locker and . . .

It was improbable. It was most unlikely. But ever since Lausanne he had been in the habit of thinking of everything, even of the most extraordinary hypotheses.

He didn't want a fortune. Not for a second had he thought of changing their way of life in any way, of leaving his job with Monsieur Baudelin, of moving to another apartment, of taking it easy on the Riviera or buying a house in the country.

He had grown accustomed to certain settings, to a

certain routine; he would have felt out of his element.

What he longed for was to be able to satisfy some small wishes he had cherished since his childhood—to buy a certain type of penknife, for instance, like the ones that old Cachot, the cutler at Gien, used to sell when he was a boy. And to buy his wife and children an occasional present.

On Sundays when they didn't go to Poissy, they liked to spend the afternoon window-shopping, joining the crowds wandering up and down the Champs-Élysées, Avenue Matignon, and Faubourg Saint-Honoré.

"Look, Daddy. . . ."

Even if it was a toy costing only a few francs, Dominique would drag Josée away.

"What would you do with it? If we were to buy everything you wanted . . ."

But Dominique herself would stop suddenly in front of a handbag or scarf at Hermès or some other shop.

It was these little things that would have given them so much pleasure and that he would so much have liked to buy for them. Without endless discussions. Without the hesitation that preceded every purchase. Open the shop door. Point to the object, without having to ask the price. . . .

He thought about the Boston burglars more and more frequently and he ended up by admiring them, finding it unjust that they should be serving a prison sentence of at least fifteen years without having touched a single dollar bill, without having had the slightest satisfaction or the hope of ever having any.

And that poor devil . . . the accomplice who had betrayed them out of weakness because, in a fit of euphoria a week before the ten years were up, he had been unable to resist his urge to behave like a rich man.

By October Calmar couldn't resist, either. He was in Gare Saint-Lazare for the second or third time. He took the case to the lavatory and opened it, with the excuse of checking whether his fortune had been replaced by old newspapers.

The bills were in place. He found another excuse for taking out a fifty-pound note. For he now needed excuses for his own benefit.

The American bills were genuine; he had tested them—or at least the one he had changed in a bank on Boulevard des Italiens was genuine. But how about the English money?

He went to a different bank. The cashier went through the same procedure and finally, without looking at him, handed him some French notes.

He didn't know where to put them. He didn't know what to do with them. He simply went into one of those bars on Rue Marbeuf, one in which he had never set foot before, and, seated alone on a high stool, he drank half a bottle of the best champagne.

It gave him no pleasure. He had plenty of money left over, even after putting a hundred-franc note into the cap of a blind man who must have had a surprise when he found it.

He simply had to find a solution. It was vital. He was sufficiently lucid to realize that he was undergoing a moral and nervous deterioration, that he was prey to panic more and more frequently, and that people looked at him with added interest.

For nearly a week he thought about the national lottery, considering the pros and cons, trying to visualize all the obstacles, all the dangers. Then, at the beginning of November, he thought he had found a way out.

He continued to take his time, almost two weeks. One Monday evening he came home, his arms filled with presents, his face deliberately radiant in spite of the fear that gripped him.

"What's the matter with you, Justin? Do you think it's Christmas?"

"Just a minute. Children . . ."

"What is it, Daddy?"

First of all, for Bib, a car that could be driven in every direction by means of a lever connected to it by a thin wire.

"Is that really for me?"

Dominique watched him, suspicious and anxious.

"And what do I get, Daddy?"

A schoolbag, which Josée had been clamoring for for two years; ever since she had started school she had had the same old bag, which by now had turned gray and crinkly.

For Dominique a broach that she had seen one Sunday in a shopwindow on the Champs-Élysées.

"That would go well with my blue suit, don't you think?" she had said.

Finally, for himself, the penknife with six different blades, a screwdriver, a corkscrew, a saw. It was made of hartshorn, just like the one he had gazed at in the cutler's shop as a boy.

"There you are, children! You can thank the horses for that. . . ."

"The horses?" repeated Dominique, who didn't dare be pleased.

"It's quite simple. On Saturday morning at the office, a client told me he had a sure tip for a race. His brother-in-law is a jockey or a trainer, I'm not sure which, at Maisons-Laffite. He asked me if I wanted to risk five francs and I gave him the money to bet for me.

"I don't know anything about horses. I don't even know the names of the horses he backed. I was amazed this afternoon when he gave me more than six hundred francs and told me we had won 'out of order.' It appears that if we had backed the same horses in the correct order we would have won more than twelve thousand francs. . . ."

Dominique relaxed a little, but remained pensive.

"I've heard that people who gamble for the first time nearly always win."

Josée was already stuffing her new bag with textbooks and exercise pads, while Bib was still trying to find out how his car worked.

"It only goes backward, Daddy. . . ."

"I'll show you. . . ."

It took him several minutes.

"I hope you don't develop a taste for it, Justin. You see, I heard such a lot about racing during my childhood. . . ."

He knew the story by heart; it was part of the Lavaud tradition. The grandfather had owned an excellent restaurant on Rue des Petits-Champs that was frequented by well-known journalists, writers, and society figures. For years the restaurant had been in fashion, and some financiers, on their way from the Stock Exchange to Longchamp, used to lunch there in their morning coats and gray top hats.

"He started by betting small sums from time to time, whenever he was given a tip. Then he wanted to see the horses, so he would go almost every afternoon, leaving the chef to run the restaurant.

"It seems that he had big winnings to start with . . . he even thought of redecorating the restaurant, which would have made it lose its character. . . .

"But unfortunately he lost his money first. Three years later my grandfather was the headwaiter in his own establishment, which had been taken over by one of his employees.

"If Daddy had inherited the business, as he would have done in the normal course of events, he wouldn't have had to work as a pageboy at the Wepler at the age of fourteen. . . ."

Calmar tried to make a joke about it, with a forced smile:

"He would never have met your mother. . . ."

His mother-in-law had been a cloakroom attendant in the same restaurant.

"My grandfather ended completely broke, going around to all his children every week in order to wheedle some money out of them. And he died at the racetrack at Saint-Cloud, of a heart attack, they say, but I'm pretty sure it was malnutrition. . . ."

He had to tread gently and carefully. Above all, he had to get something that Dominique really wanted next time. He racked his brains, trying to remember all the little phrases that women slip into the conversation about shopwindows into which they have gazed longingly.

He waited a fortnight. That Monday he didn't say anything but made a point of looking gleeful.

"Have you been gambling again, Justin?"

"Sh . . ." he murmured mysteriously, glancing toward the children.

Then, later, in bed:

"I shouldn't have said how I got the money last time in front of the children. I don't consider betting particularly immoral, but it's just as well not to talk about money that has been won so easily. . . ."

"Did you win?"

"Nothing much."

"How much?"

"Enough for me to give you a nice surprise tomorrow."

So, little by little, he built himself a vice, an "alibi-vice," as he called it.

"I think I'd rather not have a surprise."

"Look, Dominique, would you think it normal to turn your back on a sum of money within your reach—gratuitous, legitimate money?"

"I've told you what I think of betting at the races. . . ."

"Don't you ever buy lottery tickets?"

He had a good point there, because Dominique

bought a lottery ticket almost every week when she did her shopping, and, if she had the chance, she watched the drawing on television, her ticket in her hand.

"I've never won anything."

"Yes, you have. A thousand old francs four years ago . . ."

"After buying over a thousand francs' worth of tickets in the previous years . . ."

"What if you'd won the hundred million?"

"That sort of thing only happens in dreams. . . ."

"It happens to somebody every week, not to mention the other prizes."

She was talking as he would have talked before the return journey from Venice.

This time his present was a dishwashing machine and she couldn't hide her tears of joy.

"I know you wanted one. I'm going to tell you a secret. Almost every evening you miss the eight o'clock news on television because of the washing up. From now on you'll be with me. . . ."

They put the children to bed just before eight (this was Justin's job) in order to spend most of their evenings watching television.

"It's sweet of you to have thought of that . . . but you aren't going to go on, are you? How much did you bet?"

"Five francs each time . . ."

"Didn't you bet last week?"

"Five francs, which I lost. But in three weeks I've made a profit of over one thousand three hundred francs."

"Do your colleagues know?"

"My client doesn't want me to tell them, because if the news got around the odds might drop."

"Who is he?"

"Somebody I've never mentioned to you, called Leferre . . ."

"Ending in *f-e-r*?"

"No. With two *r*'s and one *e*."

From one minute to the next he had had to give a name to the character who was gradually going to come to life.

"What does he do?"

"He's a buyer for the sports department of a store in Paris. They're important customers . . . when an article succeeds with them, it'll succeed all over France. . . ."

"Why do you see him rather than Challans? I thought you were only in charge of the foreign department. . . ."

Again he had to improvise, terrified of committing a blunder, of saying the wrong sentence, the wrong word, which would entail other questions that he couldn't answer without sounding implausible.

"The first time he came to Avenue de Neuilly he was looking for new gadgets for an English department store, which he also represents. They obviously sent him to me. After that, he continued to come to me. Challans wasn't too pleased about it, of course. . . ."

"Has he got it in for you?"

"Not really. It turned out all right in the end. I sometimes take him . . ."

"Leferre or Challans?"

"Leferre, of course . . . if you go on interrupting I'll never finish. I was saying that I sometimes take Leferre to Challans' office, which is more impressive than mine, so that pompous idiot can show off his bar, offer Leferre a drink, treat him as though he were his own client and as if I were no more than an occasional go-between helping him out. . . ."

It was complicated, of course. And he realized that it would become increasingly complicated, that he would have to be on his guard to act and, above all, speak with the greatest caution.

This affected his mood. His first purchases had thrilled him. It was rather as if he had broken out of some magic circle in which he had long felt enclosed.

From now on he could have small sums in his pocket that he didn't have to justify. Leferre was always there to explain why on some days Justin's breath smelled slightly of liquor.

Because now he had a drink every day, in the morning or in the evening.

Since he couldn't go into a café near the office without being seen, and since he couldn't leave his car on the Champs-Élysées or anywhere else in the no-parking area, he planned routes that enabled him to stop for a few minutes in quiet streets.

He would go into a bar, gulp down a drink, and signal to the owner or waiter to give him the same again.

This gave him a sense of excitement, of imminent danger, of possible catastrophe, which he had experienced at the Lycée Carnot when he looked for Mimoune at the beginning of a class and wondered what sort of quarrel was brewing.

He changed bars almost every day. He did not want his face to become familiar enough anywhere for him to be taken for a regular customer.

One Saturday evening he opened the paper as obviously as he could at the racing page and, when the television commentator spoke about next day's race, he pulled his pencil out of his pocket and made some notes in the margin.

"What are you doing, Justin?"

He was preparing for the future. Clearly, Leferre couldn't come to Avenue de Neuilly every week. And Justin wouldn't be on close enough terms with him to ask for a tip on the telephone.

Of course, he didn't need big sums, he told himself, but he did want to have some pocket money, some free money.

This even helped him in his attitude toward his colleagues. For instance, when Challans strutted about like a dog at a dog show, he could address him silently:

"Throw your chest out, old man! I know you're the managing director and that your office is more luxurious than mine, that you can go away whenever you like, that you've bought yourself a modern apartment in a new building at Celle-Saint-Cloud, where the tenants have a swimming pool and four tennis courts. You earn twice as much as I do and your son is now a member of the faculty of the School of Political Science.

"In spite of all that, you can hardly make ends meet. . . . I'm sure you're in debt and that your smart tailor isn't paid regularly. . . .

"But I'm rich. I can go through that door and buy Havana cigars, I can take a single puff and then crush it under my heel. . . .

"I have as much money as I like. . . . I have so much that I don't know what to do with it, and my main problem is to find ways of spending it. . . .

"I'm rich, you hear?"

If he hadn't been superstitious he would have added: "I'm stinkingly rich!"

His wife murmured with a sigh:

"You haven't seen Leferre, have you?"

"After his last orders he won't be calling on us for another few weeks."

"Are you going to bet all the same?"

"Five francs, tomorrow morning, pari mutuel."

"Are you backing the horses recommended on television?"

"No. I take notes. I read the papers. Tomorrow morning I'll follow my own instinct."

"Aren't we going to Poissy?"

"Don't you think it's becoming rather monotonous? I don't mind going in the summer. When the weather's fine the children can play outside. But in November,

everybody sitting around a table waiting for customers . . ."

"You worry me, Justin. I don't know what's come
over you, but you're no longer the same person since
we've come back from our vacation. At first I wondered
whether you were ill and were trying to hide it from
me. . . ."

"I bet you telephoned Dr. Bosson."

"I did. He asked me a few questions—whether you
were eating and sleeping properly, et cetera—then he
told me he'd come and see you if you didn't get any
better . . . you're sure you're all right?"

"I've never felt better in my life."

He had found a solution to the problem of his breath.
He would buy chlorophyll tablets—he simply had to
get rid of any hint of liquor. Only he couldn't keep
them in his pocket when he came home, because his
wife sometimes emptied his pockets when she was
brushing his suits.

When he first started using them, he had rather
ingenuously bought a new box every day at a different
chemist and had thrown away what he didn't take.

Then he had thought of a more obvious solution.
Lately, it was often the most obvious solutions that
never entered his mind or, if they did, filled him with
astonishment: he kept the box in his desk drawer.

If anyone evinced any surprise at this he would simply reply that he suffered from heartburn and that
chlorophyll was good for him.

"All I ask you, Justin, is not to talk about horses in
front of the children."

"Of course not. Besides, tomorrow I'll place my bet
in a nearby café and say that I have some shopping to
do."

"Josée will be disappointed. . . ."

"I can hardly take her to a pari-mutuel office. . . ."

"Couldn't you just stop betting?"

"Don't you realize how little relaxation I have, darling? Would you prefer a man who chases after women or who meets his friends in a café every night for a game of billiards or a hand of bridge? I work all day . . . then all I want to do is be with you and the children. Don't you think you can allow me a little weakness, a harmless weakness?"

"I don't understand."

"What?"

"Your sudden passion for horse racing."

"Because I win . . ."

"And when you lose?"

"I'll only lose five francs a week, the price of two packs of cigarettes. . . ."

"You're right, I know. . . . I thought you were stronger-willed than that. . . ." He had succeeded: he had become a weakling!

Bob was sitting on the edge of the desk, a cigarette glued to his lower lip, his shirt sleeves rolled up. As the artist of the house, he took his jacket off as soon as he arrived, wore polo-neck sweaters in the summer and woolen sports shirts with breast pockets in the winter.

"You really are beginning to worry me, Justin, old man . . . you'll probably say it's none of my business, but you know how fond I am of you both. . . ."

"Of us both?"

"Of Dominique and you, if you'd rather. Does she know yet?"

It was one of the times when he was most frightened.

"What do you mean?"

"Listen, you ass! She's no more of a fool than I am and I guessed some time ago. Who is it?"

He really didn't understand.

"I could tell you when it started and I should have

known what was going on right off. It's so unlike you that I thought of everything except that. You must have met her during that week you spent alone in Paris, when your wife and children were still in Venice. . . .

"Unless you met her on the train . . . that's quite possible. Am I right? You met her on the train? And it's because of her that you've been so peculiar since you've been back?"

Calmar said nothing, trying to think fast, to consider the pros and cons.

"You admit it?"

"There's nothing to admit."

"You don't deny it either?"

"I have nothing to say. . . ."

"My advice to you is that it's a bit too obvious. You used to be one of the last to leave the office for lunch and you now rush out without saying good-by to anyone. You're always finding excuses for leaving early.

"The same thing happens in the afternoon. In the old days you used to have a chat with me on your way out and ask if I had my car . . . what do you say to that?"

"Nothing. I'm listening."

"Then there are your ties, which have changed. You've started drinking . . . yes, yes! Don't deny it. It's not only your breath that gives you away. It doesn't take much for a hardened drinker like me to tell when a person has had two or three drinks. . . ."

"I never have three drinks. . . ."

"Let's say that two have the same effect on you. And you suck chlorophyll tablets so that your wife won't notice. . . ."

"Have you been through my drawers?"

"I didn't need to. I've seen you slip one into your mouth and I've smelled it . . . and now your checked sports jacket."

Justin couldn't help smiling. The checked sports jacket, genuine Harris tweed, was the finest present he had been able to give himself. He had wanted one for years, ever since his adolescence. As a teacher he had had to wear rather neutral-colored suits. Here, too, he had thought it necessary, like everyone else except Bob, to wear gray or navy blue.

When he had come home with the jacket, Dominique had exclaimed:

"You're not going to wear that to the office, are you?"

"Why not?"

"That's not the sort of thing you can wear to see your clients."

"I don't see the clients. . . ."

"How about Leferre? And the others you've mentioned?"

"That's different. They come to ask my advice. They don't expect me to dress like a bank clerk or a hotel receptionist. Incidentally, now that you mention him, Leferre always wears tweed, too. . . ."

The material was both soft and rough. With a pair of dark-gray trousers, it was just the sort of thing American actors used to wear in movies where they played the part of a man to be reckoned with, independent, courageous, calm, and sure of himself.

"Who is it? One of the secretaries? Madeleine?"

He shook his head.

"Olga?"

"No."

"Is it somebody in the office?"

"I don't know. I've got nothing to say. . . ."

"Just a minute! It's not that poor Valérie, who rushes up whenever you ring for a typist. . . ."

"No. It isn't Mademoiselle Denave."

"I'm not as sure as you seem to be. Anyhow, old man, I advise you to watch out. Dominique adores you. She's a good girl who trusts you. If she ever found out that you were having an affair . . ."

Wasn't it rather astonishing that Bob should lecture him in the name of Dominique, who had been his mistress before becoming Madame Calmar?

"Don't worry. I'm old enough to know how to handle this. . . ."

"The thing is that you're the sort of guy who creates trouble for himself. As for me, I'm used to it. Women know in advance that it won't be serious, that it'll only last a few weeks and that there's no point in getting attached.

"But you're a sentimentalist, and if you get involved with a real bitch who knows how to set about it, I wouldn't answer for what might happen. . . ."

"You don't have to answer for it, do you?"

"Have it your way. I've warned you. . . ."

Bob left the office. Calmar wanted to rub his hands, the whole business delighted him so much.

At home he had the alibi of the pari mutuel. He had become the stolid man suddenly bitten by a passion for gambling and unable to do without it.

At the office he was already, in Bob's eyes (and would soon become so in everybody else's), the married man with children who was bashfully concealing a love affair.

So they could go on spying on him. In both cases his bizarre behavior and his sudden changes of mood would be attributed to one of his two vices.

Without conviction, simply because he wanted to stick to the line of conduct he had planned for himself, he continued to buy the *Tribune de Lausanne* every day at one of the four or five newspaper stands at which he knew he could find it. The day after, he was amazed to read on the fifth page:

"An Arrest in Connection with the Manicurist

"Our readers may recall that, on August 20, a young manicurist from Zurich was found strangled in her apartment on Rue du Bugnon and that the murder appeared to have been committed on the previous afternoon.

"We now know that three days ago the police arrested a Dutch national for questioning. According to the latest report he is being held in solitary confinement by the district attorney La Pallud."

Just when he was starting to relax, to relish his money in peace!

Who was this Dutch national? And didn't the fact that he was Dutch suggest an international organization?

The man with a Middle European accent on the train from Venice had been coming from either Belgrade or Trieste that Sunday.

According to that August issue of the *Tribune de Lausanne,* Arlette Staub had worked as a manicurist in hotels frequented by a cosmopolitan clientele.

"And I'm French!" he felt like adding, almost comically.

"Now, ladies and gentlemen, some sports news. Cycling . . ."

He wasn't listening. He was thinking about the Dutchman, about the chances of his mentioning the attaché case and its contents. If he did so, it was perfectly possible that, months later, the police might discover that an individual in a cream-colored suit who had taken a taxi to Rue du Bugnon, carrying an attaché case, had hurried back to the station, and had had two whiskies in rapid succession.

"Next Sunday, the first Sunday in December, the last great race meeting of the season will be held at Maisons-Laffite. We shall give our own forecast on Saturday, as usual, but for the moment it looks as though the mare Belle-de-Mai, who came second at the . . ."

He had heard all right, the last race meeting of the season. Did that mean that there would be no more pari mutuel for some time to come?

Another piece of bad news—because by now he had settled into his new routine. On Saturday evening, during the TV movie or play, he conscientiously made notes on the racing page of the paper, and on Sunday morning he went out alone, nearly always on foot.

"Which office do you go to?" Dominique had asked him.

"I change every Sunday. That's why I take the car some days and not others. If I always went to the same one they would soon notice my luck and other people would back the same horses. Besides, it's better people shouldn't know I'm winning all this money, if only because of income tax."

"Do you think one has to declare gambling profits?"

"I don't know. I'll make some discreet inquiries."

Another brick. Dominique was so scrupulous that she was quite capable of making him declare his winnings, if that was the law.

Since it was the last race meeting of the season, he was going to pull off something big, so as to get some leeway. That Sunday, after he returned home, they drove to Poissy for the first time in several weeks. Toward the middle of the afternoon he was dozing as usual in one of the bedrooms when Dominique came in.

"Justin! Can you tell me which horses you backed?"

He smiled with an effort.

"Never, darling. That's a question you don't ask a gambler. If I told you it would bring me bad luck, or I'd think it would, and I'd never pick my horses so freely and instinctively again. . . ."

"Belle-de-Mai?"

"Yes . . . it's the favorite . . ."

"Germinal?"

"Who told you about Germinal? I thought you never read the racing page?"

"I don't, but it's just been mentioned on the radio. Did you back it?"

"Perhaps."

"And Palsembleu? Answer quickly. . . ."

"I repeat: perhaps."

"If you backed those three horses in that order you've won an enormous amount of money . . . they're worth over two thousand seven hundred francs for every franc. . . ."

"That's not much."

"Look quickly. . . ."

"No point. I backed them."

"Look all the same, Justin. . . ."

She was more excited than he was. Fortunately, he always had the ticket in his pocket and his wife couldn't understand the little holes stamped against his bets.

"There you are! Belle-de-Mai, Palsembleu, Germinal, Lousteau, and Gargamelle . . ."

"You've said five names . . . and you said Palsembleu second. . . ."

"By mistake. I swear I backed them in the correct order and the fact that I backed five horses doesn't alter a thing."

"How much did you bet?"

"Ten francs . . ."

"I thought you only bet five francs a time?"

"Today I bet ten. . . ."

"So that you've won over twenty thousand francs?"

"That's right. Look, darling, do you know what you're going to do as soon as I lay my hands on the money?"

"I'm glad and I'm sorry at the same time. I'd so much rather we'd got it some other way! I can't help thinking about my grandfather. What amazes me is that you should be so calm. . . ."

"Maybe it's because I'm not really a gambler and won't really end up as badly as you feared. So tomorrow or the day after you'll go and buy yourself a nice fur coat. . . ."

"Are you mad?"

"I didn't say mink. . . ."

He added, trying to laugh:

"Or chinchilla. I don't know what you prefer . . . you once mentioned leopard. . . ."

"It's no good for the winter. And leopard is too showy . . . it's all right for women who have three or four different furs. . . ."

"Well, what else?"

"Shall I tell you my dream? Even a good quality one isn't so expensive . . . a wildcat. It's come into fashion again . . . they make some very neat, very unobtrusive ones. . . ."

"Will you also get the suit costing three hundred and twenty-nine francs on Avenue de Wagram? With the change . . ."

"With the change or, rather, with part of the change, because we must think of the future. We'll have the apartment redecorated. It's needed it for so long. . . ."

For the first time since they had come to spend their Sundays at Poissy she went to the door and, blushing like a schoolgirl, locked it before joining her husband on the bed.

"You won't gamble any more, will you? Promise?"

He had a new suit, new shoes, a new overcoat and hat, but all this gave him hardly any pleasure and he was almost ashamed the first morning he wore them at the office.

Because of Bob's joke about his checked sports jacket, he had ordered some conventional but very smart clothes and had even taken the ridiculous step of ordering them from Challans' tailor.

The children, too, all had new clothes. They talked of nothing but Christmas, as did the radio and television. There were fir trees in every shopwindow, luminous festoons hung over the main shopping streets, and a vast Christmas tree, the largest in the world, according to the newspapers, stood in front of Notre-Dame.

Dominique was thrilled with the wildcat fur; she had bought a hat to match. Placed at an angle on her fair hair it made her look softer, more fragile, more tender. She resembled those elegant women on old prints sitting in a sleigh huddled in their furs, their hands snuggly plunged into a muff.

But was she so soft and so tender?

She watched over his health, of course, and fretted whenever he appeared to be nervous or depressed. And he was constantly nervous and depressed, though he didn't know why.

It wasn't only the fear that the Lausanne episode might have a nasty ending. The bills in the attaché case had receded into the background. He changed the case from one station to another every four or five days quite automatically now, and he sometimes got confused and started driving to Gare Saint-Lazare before he remembered that he had left it in a locker at Gare de Lyon.

7

He drank for the sake of drinking and felt more and more depressed as the holidays approached.

"No, children, we can't go to the mountains. Young people may have Christmas vacations, but grownups don't...."

Bib had dictated to his sister a page-long list of presents he wanted; they included toys he had seen advertised on television.

"Now that Daddy is earning so much money ..."

To account for all their new clothes, their mother had explained:

"Your daddy has worked so hard that his boss has decided to give him a raise."

"What's a raise, Mommy?"

"More money every month ..."

"So we'll be moving out?"

"Why do you ask that?"

No doubt Bib remembered a conversation he had overheard when Dominique and her husband had been unaware that he was listening. They had often imagined, in some distant future when they would be rich, that they would buy a bungalow just outside Paris or, like Challans, an apartment in a modern building.

Josée had taken her father aside.

"Thank you, Daddy! I'm so glad that you did all this for us, but I hope it's not too exhausting for you."

After a pause she continued, awkwardly:

"Don't laugh at me if I say something silly.

"I can't help wondering ... I think of you often, you know ... whether it's true that one can die of exhaustion."

"Who told you that?"

"Nobody. But I've often heard Mother sigh:

" 'I'm dead with exhaustion ...'

"But Mother hasn't got so much work or so many

worries as you have. An office is harder than school, isn't it? And at school when we do math I sometimes feel so tired that I want to die and I wonder whether I'm going to die, with my head on the desk . . . that never happens, does it?"

"Never, darling. Whatever your mother might say when you make too much noise in the evenings, my office is no more tiring than school."

The weather was gray. It rained a great deal. The days when it didn't rain the sky was a raw-white color and a northerly wind swept the streets.

Calmar was sad. It was a vague sort of sadness and he thought more often than usual about the classes at the Lycée Carnot, about the life he had led there, which a boy named Mimoune had brought to an end.

What had become of Mimoune? Had he followed in his father's footsteps and gone into the civil service or politics? Would he be a minister one day? That was possible and that, too, pained him, for no particular reason.

There were times when the mystery in which he had to envelop everything he did filled him with excitement, even the humdrum gesture of opening the *Tribune de Lausanne.* He now wondered whether it was worth continuing to buy it.

He also wondered . . . but that was less concrete. He had only removed a few bills from the fortune stacked in the briefcase purchased on Boulevard Beaumarchais.

There was enough left to buy ten bungalows in the country or ten apartments like Challans' at Celle-Saint-Cloud. The whole family could live in a village in the south of France, where they need do nothing but go fishing.

He had never been fishing, even when he was a child, maybe because of his father's profession and his own nickname, "Maggot."

It wasn't really that he felt downhearted or discouraged. It was more like exhaustion, a sort of melancholy that he wanted to describe as cosmic.

A large town with over five million men, women, and children was surrounding him. Four times a day he entered the stream of cars that were all going somewhere, he didn't know where. Everyone was going somewhere. Everyone was in a hurry. Everyone had to work to buy this or that and the television exalted the benefits of winter sports, the joys of a cruise in the Mediterranean or elsewhere.

Ever since Venice, he disliked the Mediterranean. He had never been skiing—he couldn't see himself on a pair of skis, falling heavily every five yards to the amusement of the children.

He preferred his apartment on Rue Legendre, although it wasn't really *his* apartment since it had been given to them by his in-laws. In other words, it wasn't a Calmar apartment but a Lavaud apartment.

Dominique was a Lavaud and would remain one whether she liked it or not. The proof was her terror of gambling because of her grandfather's downfall, which might just as well have been due to bad management.

The Lavauds—or Dominique's father, at any rate—were not intelligent people. They had their own truths, their family truths, which nobody was allowed to question or doubt.

"Believe me, children. . . ."

Believe me. . . . It was peremptory, the voice of wisdom, of experience.

He was appalled by the idea of continuing to see them every Sunday and of spending Christmas day with them, surrounded by guests he didn't know but whom old Lavaud knew.

In short, he was tired, for no particular reason, because of everything in general, and he wondered whether he would go on wearing his new suit or his new overcoat, which made him feel as though in disguise.

There was only Mademoiselle Denave, the least attractive of all the typists, who looked at him with blissful admiration and rushed up to his office on the slightest excuse.

She, too, had started off by falling in love with Bob. Like Dominique! Justin wondered what it was about Bob that attracted women in that way.

He had been a bachelor, too, but he had had very few love affairs. They had rarely lasted more than a day or a week; he had had to cut them short because his partners immediately started to take things too seriously.

They would never have hinted at marriage with Bob. With Bob they were gay, vivacious, trying to please him, but Bob never took any trouble over them. He never asked them:

"Where would you like to dine?"

He took them to a restaurant of his choosing and ordered whatever he pleased. He never asked them what they wanted to do, either. He simply did it, and, when he had had enough, he just walked off.

Was Bob happy? Justin suspected that he wasn't, despite his meticulously organized selfishness.

Was Calmar himself happy? Not just since Venice and the ridiculous episode on the train—but before? He never asked himself the question, or hardly ever, and when he did he quickly thought about something else, the problems of family and office life.

It would go on and on like that. Josée, whose breasts were just starting to develop, would continue to grow, would turn into a girl demanding the right to go out in the evenings with boy friends or girl friends.

"Are you going to let her, Justin? Do you really think that's the sort of place for a young girl to go to?

You think she ought to see people who don't look after their children and let them dance until midnight?"

And how about her? When he met her what was she doing until midnight? She was going to bed with Bob. She sometimes used to stay with him all night, until it was time to go to the glove shop on Boulevard Saint-Michel, thanks to the complicity of a girl friend she was supposed to spend the night with once or twice a week.

But he had had to wait a month.

"You see, Justin, I'm not sure yet whether I love you. You're a good friend . . . I feel secure with you. You give the impression of being a man one can rely on. . . ."

And how about Bob? Had she wondered whether she loved him? No!

So from the first moment Calmar had been a potential husband and it was the prospective husband, not the man—and certainly not the prospective lover—whom she was testing.

He didn't hold it against her. He loved her. He had grown accustomed to her. He was afraid of hurting her. That was love, wasn't it?

He was also frightened of her excessively perspicacious gaze, the way she asked him embarrassing questions when he least expected it.

"Haven't they noticed a change in you at the office?"

"Why should there be a change in me?"

"You know why, Justin. I suppose it comes from all that money you won at the races . . . but I still don't understand. You'd already changed when the children and I came back from Venice . . . were you gambling then?"

"I think so . . . yes . . . I can't remember the exact date. . . ."

"Did you know Leferre?"

"Yes. I've known him for a long time."

"But he hadn't given you any tips before . . ."

"People don't necessarily have tips every week. Perhaps he didn't know me well enough. . . ."

"Have you ever won any money without telling me?"

"I can't remember, darling. If I did it can't have been much. . . ."

"But that means that you can hide things from me. . . ."

How about her? Was she sure she wasn't hiding anything, had never hidden anything during the thirteen years they had lived together?

"It's strange. . . ."

"What's strange?"

"You . . . everything. A fortnight ago I fell for it . . . all that money pouring into our hands. I told myself it would be too silly for us and the children not to take advantage of it. I admit that I was pleased to buy that fur coat. . . . I would have had to wait years for it otherwise. But now . . ."

"Now?"

"Nothing . . ."

She wanted to cry and he wanted to take her in his arms and whisper to her:

"You're right. You see, darling, it's all a lie . . . the best thing for me to do is to tell you the truth. It's too much of a burden for me. There are times when I want to shout it out to everybody, at the office, in the streets, in one of those bars where I go every day to read a Swiss paper in the lavatory.

"I'm rich, Dominique, and I don't know what to do with my money. I hardly have the right to spend it, however cautiously, and at any moment I might be shot in the head or end up in prison."

Without having done anything wrong!

He found the proof that he was running a risk in next day's *Tribune de Lausanne*.

"Unexpected Epilogue to the Crime on Rue du Bugnon

"In an earlier issue we reported the arrest of a Dutch national in connection with the murder of a manicurist living on Rue du Bugnon in Lausanne. He was being held for questioning by the district attorney La Pallud.

"After a few days' interrogation, however, the man hanged himself in his cell, with strips cut out of his shirt, without having disclosed anything.

"His name is Nicholas de V., aged thirty-five, a dealer in precious stones whose last known address was in Amsterdam.

"He was married with three children. When his wife was questioned by the Dutch police, she said that her husband's activities were perfectly regular and that he had to make frequent trips abroad on business. She didn't know where he was on August 19 but said that, as far as she knew, her husband hadn't set foot in Switzerland for over a year."

He was married, too. Three children, instead of two. He had hanged himself in his cell after cutting up his shirt to make a sort of rope!

And what if he hadn't hanged himself? What if he had been hanged? What if this had been the only way to avoid awkward disclosures?

Awkward for whom? Were there other hoards hidden somewhere, in other baggage lockers in other stations in Europe?

He was sick at heart. He had had enough. He wanted to go to the police and get the whole thing off his chest, once and for all. If he didn't do it it wasn't for his own sake, but for that of his wife and children.

He didn't even know what the penalty might be. Besides, no one would believe him. Not even Dominique would believe him. She had mistrusted him for weeks, for months. She had been spying on him, trying to catch him off guard with her insidious questions. So whom could he tell?

Bob? Bob went on joking with him when he came into his office, but he came less and less frequently, and when he cracked a joke one felt that his heart wasn't in it.

"You're almost as handsome as our resplendent managing director! What's happened to you, Justin? Have you inherited?

"By the way, you must come to dinner one of these evenings with me and my new girl . . . together with Dominique, of course. Don't worry, this one's very well brought up and doesn't use vulgar language.

"She's even too well brought up for my liking and wants me to switch off the light before she gets undressed . . . it's funny, because once she's naked she doesn't mind a bit if I turn all the lights on. Do you know what her father does? He's a tax inspector . . . excellent man to know. Too bad I can't tell him I'm almost a member of the family!"

Justin neither laughed nor smiled.

"How's Dominique?"

"Well."

"The children?"

"Very well."

"And you?"

Bob burst out laughing.

"If I believed in them I'd send you to a psychoanalyst, Justin . . . he'd certainly find you had some complex or other. I hope it's not an Oedipus complex . . . between ourselves, I never quite know what an Oedipus complex is. My ignorance . . .

"Seriously, though, you should look after your health. Everyone wonders what's happening to you. It must come out sooner or later. In the meantime remember that I'm always here and that I don't hear people's secrets only in bed. . . ."

As for Monsieur Baudelin, he didn't say anything, but looked at him out of the corner of his eye and sighed whenever he left Calmar's office. If he hated the desks at his establishment to be deserted, he also hated people to be ill or sad. One of his favorite dictums was:

"Don't complicate matters, my friend . . . don't complicate matters."

He had told Challans (because he couldn't bear to do such things himself) to fire a typist, who, for no apparent reason, would burst into tears in the middle of a dictation.

It was only a year later, after she was dead, that they had found out that she knew she had leukemia and that her mother would be left destitute. Such things do happen.

Friday. He left the office early, saying he had to go to the dentist, because he had to move the briefcase again.

Today it was the turn of Gare de l'Est. It was as though fate had decreed that no station should be near either his office or his apartment, so that, once or twice a week, he was obliged to cross the most crowded quarters of Paris.

He was particularly downhearted that evening and he almost ran into a newspaper vendor who was slipping between the cars on the zebra crossing.

He didn't have the courage to change stations. This one was already crowded with people in heavy shoes and multicolored sweaters who were taking the trains by storm. A ski scratched his cheek.

Leaning over locker number 27, he pulled the case out, went to another row, and slipped a coin into locker number 62, where he was going to leave his fortune.

He didn't look around. For some days he had yielded to a kind of fatalism and he had reached the point of wondering whether it wouldn't be better simply to leave his case, locked, in his office cupboard in order to avoid so many complications and exhausting journeys.

He would think it over during the weekend; he had got into the habit of thinking things over for a while before he actually did them.

It had become a mania. He did it without realizing it, as though he had a little mechanism in his head that was always ticking, even at night—he would sometimes wake up with a start, dreaming of a danger he hadn't yet thought of.

He shut the locker, slipped the key onto his key ring, and, just as he was straightening up, saw Mademoiselle Denave's face.

"Are you going away, Monsieur Calmar?"

The proof that he should always have been on his guard was that he was rash enough to say:

"Have you been following me?"

"Me? Of course not. Didn't you know that I take the train every night to Lagny, where I live with my mother?"

No. He had never wondered what Valérie did after office hours. She looked at him attentively and, at the same time, with a protective tenderness.

"You're quite flushed. You must have been in a hurry. I left the office sooner than usual, too. I took the subway. . . ."

He felt he needed to give an explanation. He knew that one should never explain, but he couldn't resist it. He couldn't stand her silence, the loving, stupidly loving, look on her face. It was as though she had been touched by catching him off guard like that, just as one is touched when one watches a child sneaking some jam.

"I had to accompany a friend to the station. Just as

his train was leaving, I realized that I was holding his briefcase . . . he had two suitcases already. . . ."

Had she seen him take the briefcase out of the other locker?

"I'm so pleased to see you here, Monsieur Calmar. It's not the same as at the office. . . ."

"Good-by, Mademoiselle Denave . . ."

"Good-by, Monsieur Calmar . . . just a minute! There's something I've been wanting to tell you for a long time, but I've never had the guts . . . here, in the crowd, it's easier. . . . I'd like you to know that I'm your friend, that you haven't got a better friend, and that I'd do anything to help you."

Without waiting for him to answer or react, she hurried onto the platform and disappeared among the skiers in their mountain clothes.

"Monsieur Calmar . . ."

"Yes?"

She had come into his office so silently that he hadn't even noticed her and he started. She had a pencil and pad in her hand.

"Do you remember what I said to you yesterday at the station?"

He muttered in embarrassment, looking elsewhere:

"I think so, yes. . . ."

"I'd like you to know that I meant it."

This was certainly premeditated, because she was wearing a dress he'd never seen before and she was more heavily made up than usual. If the make-up did little to improve her face, the close-fitting dress revealed a body that he had not even suspected.

"I need to talk to you, Monsieur Calmar. It's urgent. . . ."

"Go ahead. . . ."

"Not now . . . not with these doors and anyone being able to come in . . ."

She smiled at him discreetly, with complicity, certain that he understood her discretion.

"I have an idea. Today's Saturday . . . this afternoon the office will be empty. . . ."

"Unless the boss . . ."

"Monsieur Baudelin has left for Brézolles and won't be back before Monday morning. I typed the letters and the telegrams confirming the appointment."

He looked at her in consternation, wondering what she was getting at.

"You can tell your wife that you have some urgent work to do, that you have to work overtime. I've already taken care of Monsieur Challans. . . ."

"How have you taken care of him?"

"I told him that I was behind with the files and that I'd rather work for an hour or two this afternoon than stay late next Saturday. . . ."

"But . . ."

"At two o'clock?"

Anybody would have sworn that he'd been courting her for weeks and that she was at last according him the appointment for which he had been longing.

"The thing is . . ."

"I know you're worried . . . you'll see! I'll see you this afternoon."

He forgot to get the *Tribune de Lausanne* and, after having three instead of two drinks, he forgot to take the chlorophyll tablet he had put in his pocket.

"What's the matter, Justin?"

"Nothing. It's just that I have to go to the office this afternoon . . . something idiotic. We received the new Sears Roebuck catalogue this morning . . . it weighs almost two pounds this year and the boss wants me to give him a list of the latest items by Monday morning. . . ."

"Well, it's raining, anyhow."

He didn't understand what she meant.

"What would you have done at home? There's nothing worth seeing on television and I promised to take the children to tea at Clémence's."

He ate absent-mindedly, arrived at Avenue de Neuilly twenty minutes early, and asked the watchman:

"Has Mademoiselle Denave arrived?"

"No, sir. Is she coming?"

"She has some urgent work to do for me. Have you seen the boss?"

"He left at about ten this morning with Monsieur Marcel."

He paced up and down his office, worried, anxious, and acutely conscious of the absurdity of his position.

Hadn't he always been absurd, all his life, and hadn't the Maggot been a figure of fun ever since kindergarten?

He heard her steps on the staircase. He remained standing in the middle of his office and heard her rummaging around in her own office before she opened the door.

"Listen, Justin . . . I know I shouldn't call you by your Christian name, but I can't help it today. . . ."

She was nervous, overexcited, and she was fiddling with an embroidered lace handkerchief.

"You see, I can't bear to feel you're unhappy . . . you understand? I'm sure you've noticed that I love you, and you've never done anything to ward me off. . . ."

He felt he was suddenly in a thick fog. He heard the words, he understood their meaning, but he couldn't believe the whole scene was real. He wanted to scream "You're mad! You're completely mad!," take his hat and coat, and rush out into the open air to be among normal people, who wouldn't say things like that to him. . . .

"My colleagues feel sorry for me because I'm lonely, but they don't realize that you're lonelier than any of us . . . isn't that true, Justin?"

"I don't know. . . . I don't understand. . . ."

"Yes, you do, you do understand. You've been looking for someone in whom to confide for months, ever since you got back from your vacation. When one is saddled with a secret like yours it must be terrible. You must have thought of telling your wife, your friend Bob, but you couldn't. . . ."

She was so moved that her eyes were glistening; she must have been on the verge of tears.

"You started calling me more than the other secretaries. . . . You watched me. . . . Women notice these things. On several occasions you were about to tell me something. . . ."

"I assure you . . ."

"Sh! What if I told you I knew?"

"Knew what?"

"Maybe not the whole truth, but I suspect the rest of it. . . ."

"Do you think there's a woman in my life?"

"No longer! There may have been one, at the end of August or the beginning of September. You must have met her in Venice, or coming back on the train. . . .

"You've changed since you've been away. You needed money because of this woman. Forgive me, it's none of my business . . . but it's no fault of mine if I love you, if you're the only man who has ever attracted me. . . ."

She was only a yard away from him and she wept without bothering to dry her tears.

"This is what I wanted to tell you. I don't know where you got the money from, but I suspect it. Honest as you are, you're fretting your heart out less from fear of being found out than because you don't know how to pay it back. Listen, Justin . . ."

She drew closer to him, fell onto his chest. She went on, weeping:

"I have some savings I don't need because my mother and I have never needed much money. Since I'll never get married . . ."

He didn't dare draw away. He felt moved, not by what she was saying but by a sudden fit of self-pity.

"You can pay me back . . . you'll be serene again, cheerful. You know you're strong and it would be idiotic to let yourself be depressed by such a trifle. . . ."

"But . . ."

"The briefcase, yesterday, at Gare de l'Est . . ."

She looked at him through her tears and suddenly pressed her greedy, clumsy lips against his.

"Sh . . . don't say anything. You'll tell me later, won't you. We'll work out a way. . . ."

She kissed him again. In spite of her small, slim body her muscles were unexpectedly strong and they both rolled onto the carpet.

"Take me, Justin! I've been waiting for this moment for such a long time . . . please!"

He felt quite giddy. He didn't know what was going on any more. His hand felt the warm flesh of a thigh and suddenly he penetrated her. She screamed sharply.

She was a virgin, at the age of thirty-two or thirty-three. He was ashamed, but she squeezed him so tightly that he couldn't break away, could hardly breathe, in fact.

When she let him raise his head he saw a pair of man's shoes on the carpet, a pair of legs, a jacket, and finally the expressionless face of Monsieur Baudelin.

He stood up clumsily, while Mademoiselle Denave remained on the floor, her skirt up to her stomach, before she slowly pulled it down.

"Excuse me, Monsieur Baudelin . . ."

Then the full absurdity of the situation appeared to him in its true light, the absurdity of all that had happened ever since the Venice train, the absurdity of his own life, and perhaps of everyone else's.

As on the occasion when he slapped Mimoune, he didn't have time to reflect, to control himself, and he ran toward the window, opened it clumsily and jumped over the sill. It was raining. The pavement was wet. He heard a scream, almost the same scream as when he had penetrated Mademoiselle Denave, and, in the center of the confusion, a slim red figure stood out, a little girl waving her hand as she licked an ice-cream cone.